Awaken

Tim Bennett

ISBN: 978-0-9934006-4-3 (Hardback)
ISBN: 978-0-9934006-5-0 (Paperback)
ISBN: 978-0-9934006-6-7 (eBook-Mobi)
ISBN: 978-0-9934006-7-4 (eBook-ePub)

For more information about this book, please contact the author at www.timhbennett.com

Acknowledgements
Alison Taft – Editor
Sarah Quigley – Editor
Cover Design – Kit Foster
Interior Design – Polgarus Studios
Interior Crow Art - Kerry Bennett. www.kerrybennett.co.uk

To my parents, Mary and Peter, for showing me the true meaning of unconditional love and to my soulmate, Alexie, for helping me to persevere. I love you with every beat of my eternal heart.

ONE

The Virgin Mary's eyes followed me from her raised precipice as I joined the slow-moving line of pilgrims into the grotto. My damaged feet limped behind those of the sick and needy. My torn ankle ligaments and broken toes were just occupational hazards of my new hobby: drinking. My left hand was ready to brush the smooth black rock perpetually warmed by the touch of a thousand people with hope for a miracle-healing in their hearts. My right hand stayed in my pocket, clutching a bottle of absinthe with half its contents already charging through my veins. I'd poured the alcohol into a Virgin-Mary-shaped bottle, usually used for collecting the healing spring water from the many taps that lined the granite walls next to the shrine.

I ran my thumbnail up and down the threaded grooves of the bottle's metal cap, twisting it back and forth, eager to swig the remaining green alcohol and feel it burn the back of my throat. Absinthe was my favourite tipple, my own brand of Holy Spirit. It induced an instant and glorious euphoria, bringing me ever closer to the power everyone was searching for in Lourdes. Standard lager was just water to me now; only strong spirits distorted my sense of reality and I loved the unbalanced, strange world my perception took me to. It was nearly midnight on the last night of my trip before the homeward journey back to England with the sick and dying people I brought here every year for what sometimes turned out to be their last holiday, and to give them a chance to catch a glimmer of the light Bernadette had witnessed years ago.

The shrine lay in the centre of a hundred and twenty acres of gated Roman Catholic domain where women had to keep their shoulders covered and alcohol was banned unless you were a priest ready to share the blood of Christ. I turned a blind eye to that rule. There was no way anyone was going to stop me drinking. Abstinence was the most ridiculous idea. Lourdes had introduced me to a two-litre jug of beer called the Formidable. Every time I returned, I Christened my arrival with one, and every year I cursed the French for watering down their beer more and more, as I had to search deeper into the bottom of a glass for relief. The town glowed with neon signs beckoning the swarms of people to rest their weary feet, sing songs and get merry, their voices filling the streets which were home to hundreds of shops selling identical Catholic regalia in the form of anything from Virgin-Mary table lamps to lighters and the more grotesque tourist artefacts of holographic photos of a crucified Jesus whose eyes were closed one moment and then opened, risen again. Only five families own all the bars and shops in Lourdes, cornering the franchise and turning the town into a garish moneymaking machine.

The shrine was protected from the commercial world. Its power always hit me when I first arrived, wrapping everyone in its peaceful abyss. It was the most tranquil place. A cave just big enough for an altar, with an exposed underground stream running through its far left corner where Bernadette's vision had told her to dig with her hands. Three Catholic churches towered above the roof of the cave, stacked on top of each other, with a fourth underground in the middle of the domain as big as a football stadium, used for the evening candlelit procession in the event of bad weather. I smirked at the effort put into preserving people's faith as I shuffled my feet towards the wheelchair ramp which led into the candlelit grotto where a hush befell the humid midnight air, filled only by murmured prayers punctuated by the kissing of rosaries. I followed a short woman with dark Mediterranean skin and a hunched back. She held a photo of a child in her hands, bound by a rosary: the perfect example of faith. I kept one eye on the woman and the other on the black silhouette of a crow as it spread its wings, landing above me on Mary's white marble feet. It was a beautiful sight. The darkened depth of my soul was getting acquainted with the shining light of heaven.

'I see you,' I whispered. My words broke the shrine's silence and disturbed the hunched woman's prayers.

'Shhh,' she hissed.

The crow's presence intrigued me; I knew little about the nocturnal habits of birds. I'd never known anything other than an owl to fly at night. If there was one bird that held my attention more than any other, it was the crow. For as long as I could remember, their blackness had always distracted me from the task in hand, but that was nothing compared to the effect its 'caw' had on me. The presence of my friend on his holy perch made me smile, momentarily dispersing the cloud of impending doom gradually enveloping my life. My fingers twisted the cap, eager to sneak my final swig, but there was a hint of panic, lurking, ready to pounce as soon as the bottle was finished. Craving dug into my brain, twisting… twisting.

I watched the lady with the hunched back brush her fingers against the stone and then press them to whispering lips. Her eyes were tightly closed, stretching the creases at the corner of her eyes to the lines spreading from her constantly smiling mouth. She was in heaven, at one with her loved ones, held by God, or Mary, or Jehovah. For all its tack and glutton for financial gain, Lourdes never discriminated against other faiths. That's not to say things didn't get unpleasant when ten thousand gypsies descended on the town each year. I placed the palm of my left hand on the rock. I had no words ready for prayer, my head wanted to be soothed by alcohol, but as I moved away from the stone and placed my hand over my heart, three words escaped from my lips.

'Please help me,' I said.

I walked down the descending wheelchair ramp towards a spare stretch of bench, unwilling to acknowledge the sudden absence of the chronic pain I lived with every day in my feet. I credited the absinthe for the sudden anaesthetic effect, not a higher power living inside a mountain. My disabled traveller was tucked up in bed, on the last evening of Lourdes. A night which was usually a very special occasion for me and my wife, Karen. A chance for us to bond and soak up the extraordinary atmosphere of the quietened shrine as its visitors trickled away into the night. But this time I sat alone and full of hatred for myself. I checked my inside-pocket for the divorce papers. I always kept close to my chest to make sure they stopped my broken-heart healing.

The crow preened his feathers, occasionally checking I was still in my place. I raised the bottle of Mary to him and gave him a secret cheers with my holy water, miraculously turned green by the hand of God. I put the bottle in my pocket and pretended to pray. My nails found the cigarette burns in the palms of my hand and picked at the scabs. It was a relatively new habit of mine. Easy to do and conceal as the deranged voices inside my head kept telling me I wasn't capable of loving anyone. I withdrew into my selfish skin and drew blood from my right hand as I peeled off the scab and flicked it away, and then turned my attention to the wound in my left hand, self-inflicting my own stigmata. I pushed my index finger into the hole in my palm as the church clock struck twelve and time for a night-cap began to run out. 'Fuck it!' I said, as the pain hit me. I stared at the silver crucifix on the altar. I was in danger of getting turned on by swearing in front of the Virgin Mary. The Devil was near.

The absinthe bolstered my normally absent courage, loosening my tongue, freeing emotions and feelings I was unfamiliar with. My own Holy Spirit moved in mysterious ways once it entered my bloodstream, adding to the blur of credit cards, brandy, marijuana, beta-blockers, anti-depressants, cocaine and porn. Not ideal behaviour for a social worker. I was having an absolute blast, in secret, but I hated our little cottage with its ghouls which appeared from the wardrobe when I came down from a bender, and the constantly creaking floorboards whenever I was alone in the house.

As the clock struck a quarter-past twelve, the crow left Mary's feet, swooping inches from my head. I closed my eyes to savour his closeness as his wings moved the thin wisps of receding hair on my scalp. I was hit by a momentary burst of sadness followed by the strongest desire to get as fucked up as possible.

I swigged the empty holy water bottle to inhale any lingering fumes. I searched my memories for the good times I'd had with Karen. I knew they were there, but chemicals numbed my emotions as my senses went into overdrive, widening their radar beyond the walls of the domain for more alcohol. I left my seat in front of the grotto. The domain was ghostly quiet, and the crow flew on ahead of me, hopping along the line of taps, and then up fifty feet to the head of a saintly statue which lined the giant wheelchair ramps leading up to the three churches. He hovered above its white marbled head before making the softest 'caw', dropping his feet onto the head. The crow moved on to the next statue repeating his landing with a slightly louder 'caw', descending onto the last one at ground level where he waited until I'd reached the feet of the statue. He hopped excitedly as I approached.

'Caw!' he said.

'What do you want, little fella? I'm not the greatest company at the moment and I've got no booze left. Wanna join me for another?' I turned my back on him and headed for the nearest bar.

'I told you not to marry her,' a voice said.

I looked around, but no one was there, except for a monk in a classic brown cassock and leather sandals walking silently past me to the shrine.

'Wh... who said that?' I stuttered.

'I did, over here,' the voice said again. I looked behind the statue with no clue as to what or who I was expecting to find. My head buzzed with a mixture of euphoria and dread. The only thing that could quell the confusion was another absinthe, a leveller to take away the dread and send me into orbit for a few more hours before I needed to get back to the hotel and turn over Joel, my disabled companion, to prevent him from getting bedsores.

'Pssst, up here,' the voice called.

I looked up to the top of the statue where the crow sat. He looked down with his head cocked to one side.

'What took you so long,' Crow said.

'I thought Bernadette was the only one who had apparitions round here,' I said.

Crow flew off to the larger-than-life-size statue of Mary facing the front of the three churches. It was a spooky statue; everyone was mesmerised by Mary's face, even sober people, even priests. Her smile twinkled, greeting whoever came to say hello.

'What is it with you and Mary?' I said, catching up with him as he sat on her feet.

'What is it with you and Karen?' Crow said, with a hop and a spread of his wings.

'What the hell are you talking about?'

'Why did you hurt someone you love so much? I could see it coming a mile off, don't you remember the broken window at the church on your wedding day?'

I flashed back to that morning as I fixed my cufflinks and the thud I heard on the sacristy window. A zig-zagged crack appeared in the glass with just the smudged silhouette of a bird with its wings spread wide in a 'woah, shit!' pose.

'That was you?' I said, sitting down on the ground.

'I was trying to get you out of there – for her protection, not yours!' Crow said.

'I used to know myself, Crow, but I don't think I know much anymore. Only how to kill everything.' I put my head in my hands. I heard Crow's wings take off but kept my head on my knees, wallowing in my shit for a little while longer: nice warm shit.

'Caaawww!' Crow called loudly from a row of

buildings away to my left. He was standing on the top of an open wooden door which led to a lit room: the only room in the domain left open twenty-four hours a day. The Room of Miracles.

Since Bernadette had started seeing the apparitions in 1858, seven thousand cures of sick people who drank or bathed in the spring water uncovered by her have been reported. Doctors classified sixty-nine of those cures as miracles, not able to be explained scientifically in any way. The last miracle took place in 1989. I followed Crow's cue and entered the small box-shaped room. Framed photos of the sixty-nine individuals lined the walls. Once my eyes had adjusted to the transition from night to artificial light, I went to the last miracle cure and started reading the doctor's account of how a woman with half a pancreas, life-threatening blood pressure spikes and recurring tumours was healed. My eyes couldn't make it to the end of the first line, as they flicked to the other photos of the healed, their eyes staring, patronising me.

'You could have the right to be on this wall one day,' Crow said, hopping between the top of the double doors.

'You think I need healing?' I said, trying to focus as my eyes filled with green fog.

'Denial isn't just a river in Egypt, Aaron.'

My drunk brain was slow on the uptake. 'You cheeky little sh…'

'Rock bottom is a long way down, Aaron. Not everyone makes it back, my friend.'

'I can't hear you, what makes you think you're my

friend?'

'I'm the only friend you've got right now.' Crow flapped his wings and flew away into the dark domain. The suddenness of his exit left me alone, and the patronising eyes stared me out of the room. Crow was nowhere to be seen. Craving grabbed my empty stomach in its fist. How could I have been sidetracked by that little room when there was so little to believe in, let alone miracles. Nearly one o'clock in the morning: the bars would soon be closed, and the enthusiastic singing of groups of pilgrims, high on helping people, was quietening down. I tried to walk quickly across the vast expanse of concrete in front of the churches where two thousand people gathered for the candlelit processions every night of the year before they shut the gate, but the pain in my feet returned, slowing me to the pace of a cripple.

The huge ornate black gates blocked my path to the meeting with the green lady and another dose of her intoxicating blood. I pressed my forehead against the iron, hard, until it hurt. Then a tap, and another, increasing the force and tempo of the blows, as I reached a crescendo of headbutting the small ridge of one of the bars.

'Fuck... fuck... fuck,' I cursed with every blow of my head against the metal. A car with a sports exhaust tore around the corner, windows open, blaring ACDC through the streets. '*I'm on a highway to hell, a highway to hell, and I'm going down, I'm going down.*' Cigarette smoke and shrieking exploded from the windows as it passed me, a message of doom from the devil. He was near. Blood trickled down my forehead into my eyes, turning the streetlights misty red. I started my walk to the other side of the domain; the adrenalin I'd used while assaulting the gate had crashed my absinthe buzz. My palms began to sting. My ankle kept folding under the weight of my stride – penance for my award-winning clown performance at a wedding where I'd danced inebriated in front of the hot backing singers of a band, hopping, tequila'd up to the gills, charging on cocaine, the one-legged legend of the dance floor. I thought I looked like John Travolta, my foot looked like it needed amputation. But it was all right; these were just everyday drinking hazards. My drug use was still within recreational levels. I was having fun – on my own, but it was fun.

The home stretch to the last gate took me alongside the top of the underground basilica. All that was visible on the surface was the most pristine softly domed area of grass I had ever seen. Grown from celestial grass seed and watered by angels. Trespassing was forbidden, as was smoking, but I was past caring about rules and lit up a cigarette to give me a rush. Smoking after drinking absinthe on an empty stomach had some kind of catalytic effect on me; the two thousand chemicals of the cigarette mixed with whatever was in my blood to give me a burst of euphoria and confidence which was addictive in its own right. I sucked the tobacco as hard as I could and it was gone in seconds.

'Yeeeeaaahhh,' I exhaled.

'Pssst, Aaron, over here,' Crow said.

I stopped and scanned the trees and railings around

me. 'Where are you?'

'Over here!' I followed the voice into the centre of the grass dome. Crow was standing in the middle of the pristine football pitch. 'Come and join me,' he said.

'I can't, I'll get arrested,' I said.

'Breaking the rules doesn't seem to bother you these days. So a chicken can't sit with a Crow? We're both birds now, I guess.' Crow was taunting me, and it worked. I gingerly made my way over the spiked fence to avoid impaling one up my anus. I couldn't grip the railings fully with my hands, and the failing alcohol buzz sapped my confidence to leap over the waist-high fence sideways. I took off my shoes and socks, savouring the velvet shag-pile grass as I went to join Crow, in blatant view of the security guard due to walk by on his next circuit.

'I thought you'd gone for good,' I said, sitting down cross-legged a foot away from Crow. Immediately I was struck by his size. His legs were as thick as my thumbs, and his seamless feathers, silky and dense, flowed from the top of a head the size of a tennis ball. 'You seem bigger than a normal crow – are you sure you're not a raven?'

Crow hopped onto my knee, his beak suddenly at stabbing distance from my eyes. He turned his head to the side, so that his eye glared directly into mine. In the middle of the black marble-size eye I caught a glimpse of fire burning. 'Call me a raven again and I'll eat both your eyes,' he said.

'What've you got against ravens?'

'Nothing, I have a strong sense of identity, but you

wouldn't know anything about that, would you? You're losing yourself. Don't you remember anything about us, Aaron?'

'Whaddaya mean, *us*?'

Crow disappeared into thin air, and sparks of light lingered all around me, flicking my skin, triggering waves of mega-goosebumps briefly lifting the skin from my body. I squinted my tired eyes, one at a time, to make sure I wasn't missing him, but he had vanished. What did he mean *us*? I scoured my mind unsuccessfully for memories of the relationship he'd hinted existed, but my head was a dark and foreboding place I rarely felt like venturing into alone. A dancing torchlight on the grass pulled me back to the present with a shock of adrenalin. A security guard walked the path, checking the roof of the basilica. Crow had set me up like a sitting duck. I imagined him laughing in the shadows. The torchlight moved in smooth arches towards me, and I froze, preparing myself for the confrontation as the light drifted across my feet, then returned further up my legs and then my body, not stopping, just passing over me every few seconds like the beam of a lighthouse. Each time the light passed, I caught a glimpse of the guard, twenty feet away, looking right through me. He walked on.

I sat there mesmerised by my invisibility. How could he miss me like that? I started checking that my skin was still solid, patting my legs, wiggling my toes to find physical sensation. I stared at my hands, and stopped. The deep holes in the centre of my palms oozed blood and ash.

I lay back on the grass savouring my new super-power of invisibility, even though I had no idea how I'd done it. I fumbled for another cigarette to singe the wounds closed.

The grass held my body, starved of sleep, and I drifted. I spread my arms out wide and opened my palms to the sky. I turned my head to the side, thinking how nice it would be to slip away and die, right there. My body would be well looked after in such a holy place. I would be remembered for something then. People would talk about the man who died in a crucifix pose on the roof of the underground church. I could be famous for the way I died.

'Go on, just take me,' I whispered.

As I drifted in and out of consciousness I rubbed my palms on the cold dew forming on the grass to soothe my burns. The stars, so far away, felt like a good place to go. To leave this world and become an anonymous speck of light in some distant galaxy where my misdemeanours and pain could be forgotten – but I was too heavy-hearted to fly. I relinquished any power I had and plummeted downwards, effortlessly, into the darkness. The further I could get away from everyone the better they'd be. I didn't have the inclination to save myself. My head raced with cravings, and the urgency to call a dealer as soon as possible in preparation for my return home. I squinted at the sky; Crow did a fly-by. A shooting star followed his tail. I tried to think of a wish. Nothing came to mind.

I closed my red eyes and waited for a prod from a security guard's foot to rouse me from the dream I'd slipped into – or was it a dream? Instead of stars I was looking at a ceiling, illuminated by the dancing glow of candlelight. My arms, held tightly by my sides by a soft woollen blanket, could escape if they wanted to, but I felt contained and safe. Slow breathing, exhaling the pungent smell of garlic across the bridge of my nose. Hands suddenly obscured my view of the ceiling as they covered my eyes; five fingers touched my left cheek, but only four, my right. Her palms, briefly cold and clammy from having had a fresh wash, began to heat up with a ferocity I felt sure was going to blow-torch the eyeballs from my sockets. I waited for the excruciating pain of burning, but it never came. Instead the heat sank below my skin, into my cheekbones, melting every hint of tension in its path. The tips of my fingers and toes tingled with an energy which climbed up my arms and legs until I was full of a billion fireflies. All sensation of her hands disappeared, and with it the heat turned to menthol-cold with a bite so refreshing I expected to see my breath fill the room. But I knew where I was and I had no need to explore my surroundings and risk disturbing my vision. Margaret was the only woman I knew with a missing finger, the first healer I'd found with scars from wounds which held a powerful empathy for anyone who found her. Perhaps it was fate which led me to her?

All my efforts to find someone to teach me Reiki had brought me back to her door, months after denying myself the opportunity to meet her because I thought she lived too far away. I'd lost count of the number of times other teachers cancelled my appointments at the last minute: people I'd chosen because they lived near me. I was in danger of developing an inferiority complex and dispelling the notion that there was a gift inside me. The gift my friend, Mystic Mike, had told me about late into the evening of a wedding reception.

My dream instantly fed me the moment Mike's magnetic green eyes called me aside. 'Aaron, when I saw you drumming at that party you were surrounded by the most amazing green aura; there's something special about you, Aaron. I don't know what it is, but you have to check out Reiki!' Mystic said, his eyes beaming their message straight to the antenna at the centre of my forehead.

The rest of that night faded. I woke the next day to blow endless rivers of snot clear from my stinging nostrils. Mystic's words clung to me, contrasting with the drab embarrassing memories of dancing like a buffoon. I knew most people danced like fools at weddings, but I'd chosen three small steps leading to the dance floor to perform on. The bride had made it clear she didn't want anyone bringing cocaine to her wedding – or maybe that was another wedding? All were cloned with intoxication, but this one stood out because of my conversation with Mystic. It wasn't just the impact of his unfaltering sincerity that had empowered me to find someone to teach me about cosmic energy. He'd stirred my sleeping spirituality that night.

I regained consciousness on the grass to feel urine run down my thighs. Its warmth soothed me back to sleep. I felt my body sink through the grass into darkness, followed by a full body-spasm which flicked my back off the ground. As I thumped back onto the ground the dream took me back to Margaret's house. She stood in front of me as I sat in an old wooden armchair with my hands held in prayer over the centre of my chest. Her wise green eyes stared at me from a face weathered by years of working on boats and sailing around the world. Margaret had lived a life which earned her the title 'Indestructible'.

Cancer, polio and depression had paid her visits, but she never lay down to die. I sat in front of the most perfect example of a wounded healer, ready to be initiated into Reiki, but the screen went black. All vision lost.

'Wake up, wake up now!' A French foot pushed into the small of my back as daylight shocked me into consciousness. A wooden truncheon poked me in the stomach, bursting the breath from my lungs.

'Okay, okay,' I gasped, covering my cold wet crotch with my hands as a feeling of dread and embarrassment hit me like a freight train.

'You have two choices and only ten seconds to make a decision, you hear?' his pouting lips said, pushing a bushy moustache up into his nostrils. He snorted through the bristles like a bull ready to kill the matador. The truncheon pushed deeper into my stomach, squashing my bladder into submission as my crotch warmed up with a second wave of urine. 'Come with me to the police station, or run for your life.'

I knocked the truncheon out of the way and sprinted,

pulling my grass-stained tee shirt as far over my crotch as possible. A group of early morning nuns gasped as I leapt over the forbidden railings into the street. Vomit started to rise from my stomach as I ducked into an alleyway to hurl bile onto the walls. Church bells tolled: one, two, three… I held my breath as I should've been at the hotel to get Joel ready for the seven o'clock departure to the airport… eight, nine, ten. I slumped on the floor, gripped the small amount of hair I had left with my fist and ripped it out – a fitting punishment for my sins. I looked up through the narrow walls of the alleyway to a shard of blue sky as I sank through the chimney, to hell.

I returned to an empty hotel; the group had left without me. 'Monsieur, a letter for you.' The receptionist beckoned as I tried to slip into the elevator unnoticed. She handed me the envelope at arm's length to stay away from the smell coming from my damp trousers.

The note was from the doctor leading our group: 'Joel had a seizure this morning, Aaron. He needed emergency treatment in England, you'll have to make your own way home.'

I felt myself being torn apart, one half confident that the end of my life was right on schedule, the other trying to scream out in pain.

The journey back to England was riddled with panic. Rather than use the roller wheels of my small suitcase, I clutched the bag to my chest for bullet-proof protection from attacks of impending doom randomly ambushing me as I waited in the check-in queue. I called on Dr Daniels many a time during the flight. His alcoholic beverage still managed to give me the medicinal shivers as I glugged the brown syrup until the flight attendant told me I'd finished the plane's supply. I felt disappointingly 'with it' as the captain announced our landing.

The airport taxi returned me to our South London home in a suburb I'd come to know as Winebarsville. I took a deep breath and walked as normally as possible to the house, finding solace from my increasing paranoia behind the locked front door of our home. I stood panting with my back pressed to the door, so relieved that I'd escaped the police sirens. There, on the doormat, was a brown envelope with five grams of cocaine in it, pushing my bill to the dealer over the five-hundred-pound mark. The sight of tightly packed rectangles of paper charged me with excitement, blasting any anxiety out of my nervous system. I drew the curtains against my prying neighbours. The terraced house was in a narrow road with mature beech trees interspersed with street lights. I was never sure how effective the curtains were, but after I got high any concern of being seen hoofing drugs and pouring pints of wine faded fast.

I enjoyed the twilight zone that drink and drugs created. To be far removed from reality was bliss. I could be whoever I wanted to be, do whatever I wanted to. Protected by my impenetrable fantasy bubble I was sex on legs with no one to get horny with but myself. I showered repeatedly, snorting and shooting gin before going to the kitchen to pour a bottle of olive oil over my awesome body. I put on a show for the old granny who lived at the back of our house, writhing in ecstasy, but forgetting that olive oil on kitchen lino became a death trap. I slipped with such speed, my feet were above my head before I knew it. I fell in a twirling motion usually associated with Olympic divers leaping from the top board. I would've scored at least a six point two for artistic impression had I not impaled my ribs on the granite worktop on my way down to the floor. I made rock-bottom look sexy, not. Groaning on the floor, grateful for the stupid amounts of recreational anaesthetic I'd consumed, drops of water spat on my face from the ceiling as most of the water I'd showered with leaked through the floor to perform Chinese water torture on me. A crackling sound came next, as the water found the spotlights, smoke poured from the bulbs and sparks began to fly around the ceiling as it turned to charred black. I leapt to the fuse box to flip the trip switch and ended up sitting in darkness, my legendary status in tatters.

Mopping up a kitchen full of olive oil and water in the dark was a challenging task, buzzing my nuts off. But one I managed as well as could've been expected. No amount of frantic friction managed to remove all traces of my self-basting. A faint slippery sheen remained on the floor, throwing me off balance whenever I got to my feet to wring out the towels. I started rehearsing my Monday morning phone call to work. I'd perfected a forlorn tone of voice very well, but I was running out of excuses, or so I thought.

I decided to throw in the olive-oil-soaked towel and retire to the sofa for a final fat line and a spot of pillow talk with Jack Daniels before the room turned into a merry-go-round. The television came alive with MTV hot chicks in bikinis washing cars right before me on the carpet. I couldn't resist joining them. The legend was back!

I hadn't lost consciousness for very long before the first note of an evil dawn chorus brought me back to the room. The MTV girls had gone without leaving their phone numbers. Dr Daniels had signed off, forgetting to leave me with a repeat prescription. As I reached for a swig of whisky, pain lanced me in the ribs. I rolled off the sofa, flipping the contents of a full ashtray over me, and writhed in pain from the broken ribs caused by the previous night's acrobatics.

I peeked through the curtains hoping to see Crow waiting to escort me to my parents' house. I was greeted by three pigeons sitting on the branch of a holly tree a few feet from the window. As soon as they saw me their necks started flicking back and forth excitedly. Then I heard a sound so evil I thought the devil had possessed the stupid grey birds. At first they started chuckling softly, before gathering momentum, louder and louder, sporadically spreading their wings in an attempt to stop falling out of the tree. My work was done here, a spectacular effort at personal degradation complete.

TWO

I woke to the sound of a newspaper clattering through the letterbox, followed by searing pain from the broken glass that pierced my feet. Consciousness had found me again. I screwed my eyes shut, unwilling to face the light of another new day I'd prayed would never come. Why wouldn't my heart stop beating? What did it want from me? I'd hit it with more drugs and alcohol than I thought it could handle, but it wouldn't do the decent thing and stop beating. It pounded relentlessly inside my chest. A drum beckoning me back to the land of the living I had so much resentment for, a world which would surely have no use for my shit-smudged soul.

Footsteps walked past the house on the pavement as the sun put on its smug hat again, smiling through the gaps in the curtains, asking me to get out of bed for another pointless day. I hid myself away inside my parents' home. A house they had worked hard on all their lives and which I tried my best to destroy by drinking, smoking and snorting weapons of self-destruction into a body withering under relentless abuse. Their home lay in a cul-de-sac of thirty detached houses. My dad's pride and joy, expertly renovated by himself and builders he couldn't help but offer his extensive construction knowledge to. There would always be something to do around the house to occupy the ambling hours of retired life. The wipe board in the garage listed his pending jobs. Psychosis twisted everything written on it into a plot to kill me. The loft, kitchen sink, lounge cupboards and spare room were places an IRA terrorist had planted bombs to rid the world of me. Paranoia peaked as I scuttled away from the mess the three pigeons found so amusing. Flashes of the wet kitchen ceiling and furniture drenched in olive oil hit my head. I was losing the battle to keep the dread at bay.

My obsessive on-off tampering of the gas and electricity continued here in an attempt to foil the terrorist's plans, resulting in a callout to the emergency services.

'His parents are away. The fireman said he looked twitchy, like he's losing the plot or something,' I heard a neighbour say as he passed the house, nosily trying to see what was going on inside.

During the month following my return from Lourdes, I'd had an absolute blast on my own. Trips out to meet my dealer, high on cognac, kicked adrenalin into me as I ran the gauntlet, daring the police to stop me. I'd managed to avoid them and all of civilization, as I careered out of control – until last night, when two fire engines unravelled their hoses on the driveway in readiness for the fire that was a figment of my sick imagination. My head replayed the sequence of events from my nervous wait outside the house at three a.m. I wore tracksuit bottoms and a shrunken denim jacket buttoned in the wrong holes, as I talked to a big plant in the driveway.

'I know you're in there,' I said to the trembling leaves.

I tried to roll onto my side, but my broken ribs didn't want me to forget the pain I'd caused them. My tangled body lay under the duvet, soaked in sweat from compulsive writhing, which was impossible to stop. At night the bedroom came alive with phantoms and ghouls, moving out of the shadows, tying my dressing gown into a straitjacket to cart me off to the secure unit that my doctor had told my parents was available for me. I thumped my fist against my chest, angry at my heart.

'Why won't you stop beating?' I whispered.

It refused to listen. What did it want from me?

The lure of a pint of red wine tempted me out of the bedroom. I walked hunchbacked to the bathroom sink to brush the fur out of my mouth. I shut my eyes as I swilled toothpaste around my mouth, hiding from my reflection.

Craving grabbed me again. I licked my chapped lips in readiness for my liquid breakfast. Bloodstains on the carpet stopped me in my tracks. Pain shot into my feet as my steps pushed the splinters of glass deeper. Cracked ribs, broken toes, ruptured ankle ligaments, bleeding bowels: just the occupational hazards of a junkie. My heartbeat quickened and stuttered, mistimed, confused.

'Just leave me alone,' I whispered. But it thumped on.

I lay scrunched in a ball on the bathroom floor, picking the glass out of my feet. My palms were raw from burns. I used them as spit-filled ashtrays, chain-smoking through the night. I tried to sacrifice myself to God or the Devil, self-inflicting stigmata, but neither of them wanted me. I closed my eyes and tried to cry. Nothing happened.

I walked downstairs on my heels to keep the blood off the carpet, clamouring along the walls, craving drink. I held the pint of wine in front of my face to block out the reflection of my gaunt face in the kitchen window and gave a toast to myself, wobbling, teetering on the brink. I knocked it back and fell to the floor as shivers ran up my spine before relief washed over me. My hands fumbled a wrap of cocaine onto the worktop. Gone in one sniff. My nostrils burned to numbness. I moved outside for the first nicotine hit of the day, easing the chain off the side kitchen door with all the caution of a burglar to avoid drawing any neighbourly attention and prompting awkward conversations across the garden fence. As I looked across the grass I froze; my heart almost decided to pack up from the shock.

The toaster was in the middle of the garden. A few feet away, the portable radio lay in pieces. Plugs and electric cables were strewn over the garden bench, along with several screwdrivers and a hammer. The cigarette fizzed as I sucked it with all my might. Several light bulbs littered the flowerbeds and slowly the flashes hit me, reminding me of how I'd cleared the house of homemade IRA bombs the night before. The terrorist sniggered in the herbaceous border at the end of the garden. I needed more than Dutch courage for this; I fled back into the house for more cocaine to try and make my heart explode.

'You're gonna get it now,' I whispered.

'Caw!'

Just before the door shut I glimpsed his blackness fly past me a few feet from my head. I slammed the door. He stood on the toaster in the middle of the garden and let out another huge 'Caw!' He remained still for a moment and hopped into the flower bed to pick up a snail. With a few flaps of his wings he came straight for the window, tapping his load against the glass and pulling away at the last minute to avoid collision. He returned to the toaster. 'Caaaw!' I was mesmerised and it was then I noticed he hadn't always been so lucky with his aerobatics as I spotted perfect smudges of his body, beak and outspread wings imprinted on the glass. I leant over the kitchen sink and peered into the flowerbed below the window to see the collection of snails, stones, clothes pegs, chestnuts and a couple of hole-pecked Coke cans which triggered a dream-like memory of something rattling into my bedroom window above the kitchen.

Crow hopped off the toaster to rummage through the dismantled radio with his long black beak. He retrieved something and immediately took flight, flying away before making a swooping curve to accelerate toward me; he was carrying a battery. I backed away, uncertain whether the window would survive the impact. Thud! He smacked into the window and disappeared again.

The cocaine, red wine and cigarette hit my frazzled nervous system. I'd lost all tolerance for substances, granted only a few minutes of good-time buzz before anxiety set in. I crept to the front lounge to see if Crow had changed his angle of attack, but he'd gone, replaced by three pigeons pecking away at moss growing on the brick driveway.

The pigeons began their morning cooing, while my head translated the rhythm of their soft sounds into manic shrieking, 'You promised her, Aaron, you fucking promised her you'd stop!'

My head bobbed up and down from the sofa every few minutes to check the driveway. I looked for something to distract me from the fear. Remembering I'd stashed some pornographic magazines under the sofa, I pulled one out, but my eyes turned every word from English to Spanish. The attempt to satisfy my failing carnal desires triggered another in a long line of house searches, this time not for explosives but for the greasy Spaniards responsible for switching my porn. They dodged me every time I checked under a bed or in a wardrobe. The searches were intense and physically exhausting. Paranoia wouldn't let me rest until I'd covered the whole house two or three times over. No Spaniards.

I sat on the lounge rug; glass crunched under my arse. Peeling back the rug I found the cause of my cut feet. The lounge was scattered with biscuits from a missing tin that rattled into the conservatory windows. The shock made me ever so slightly shit myself.

As if being besieged by a food container wasn't enough, my phone rang, a sound programmed into my brain to expect the drug dealer to say he was on his way. Like Pavlov's dog expecting his food, I answered without thinking about how I could possibly talk to anyone about anything, other than how to get more drugs.

'Heo?' I said, the ability to use consonants lost in my gurning jaw.

'Can I speak to Aaron Blake, please,' a familiar voice replied.

'Hi, yeh,' I said, suddenly recognising my manager's voice. What would be my latest explanation for being off for the longest absence since the start of my social-work career?

'Aaron, this is Frank. How are you doing?'

'Oh, hi Frank, I'm still not doing that great. I need to see my GP again. I'm not sure the anti-depressants are working, he's prescribed me beta-blockers. I thought you might have been him, actually – his receptionist said he would call me back. I don't know when I'm going to be able to come back to work, I'm really sorry, is everything okay with my caseload?' I rambled on.

'We're worried about you, Aaron. Don't worry about your cases – are you okay?'

'I don't know, Frank. I don't know what's going on. I haven't talked to my wife in weeks.' I tried to cry again, to release the flood gates. Someone asking me if I was okay was a lifeline, a chance to scream out and say, 'No, I'm not okay, I'm in deep shit, I'm dying, I'm going fucking insane, please help me!' but the courage wasn't there.

'Listen,' Frank said. 'I know you're having a hard time at the moment, but we need to know whether to bring in cover for your caseload, so let me know if your doctor signs you off for longer – by the end of next week. Take care of yourself.'

'Thanks, will do.' I couldn't muster any more words; I hung up and gasped for breath.

I'd worked with disabled children for nearly twenty years and as a social worker for the last ten, I had been promoted two years earlier – but whatever they'd seen in me had vanished.

My dad's Great Britain road atlas called out to me from the bookshelves. I'd stared at it a hundred times, trying to muster the courage to find my way to Beachy Head and drive as fast as I could over the edge. Sending my metal coffin as far away from land as possible to make my body vanish and spare my parents the cost of a funeral – but I had no courage left.

I dragged myself upstairs to drink half a pint of the cheapest corner-shop whiskey stashed under my mattress. As the lights behind my eyes went out, the whispering shadows closed in on me, ready to tie me up with the piss-stained dressing gown. My relentless heart kept beating.

Crow tip-tapped across the roof tiles of the garage, sensing my demise. He'd done his best to wake me from every drunken stupor of the last month. The pauses in between the pigeon's psychotic screams were occasionally occupied by his caw, momentarily stopping their shrieking. The pigeons tried to send me further away. Crow's caw brought me back, asking me to remember the light which had once shone so brightly on my life, asking me to see I had a choice. He waited patiently, watching over me devotedly, my black satin sentry.

The effects of my breakfast kept me unconscious and out of trouble for the whole day. I woke at dusk with the memory of being raped by the shadows. I felt violated and filthy. I stared at the bedroom ceiling, a room I'd first used when I was eleven years old. I'd always felt spooked as a child. Night-times were often terrifying and now I found myself back in the same room filled with fear as another 'dark night of the soul' began to rear its ugly head.

My earliest memories of sleeping were screaming for company from my cot to quell nightmares brought on by breathing in the dark corners of the bedroom. I'd wake to see the silhouette of a Victorian lady kneeling by my bed, her hair towering above her head. I spent many a night sleeping on the floor outside my parents' bedroom, seeking solace in the comfort of their mortal presence. A vicious circle completed itself as I lay petrified, waiting for whatever the coming hours would bring.

I scoured the bedroom for something drink, forgetting about the mirror on the wall. It grabbed my reflection and held me still as I came face to face with features I no longer knew. I leant forward to take a closer look, a first real look at my bloodshot eyes and cheekbones jutting out from a face, gaunt from the chemical barrage.

The bridge of my nose had raw dents in it from being repeatedly rammed by the edge of a glass. A shadow crept over my soul. I felt so far away.

I don't know how long I stood there for. A magnetism held me; I was plugged into a memory that flowed back to remind me of what happiness was. I was ten years old in the South of France, standing on my dad's clasped hands in the shallow end of a swimming pool, its surface sprinkled with ash from distant forest fires. I looked into his big kind brown eyes, his breath warm against me as he said softly with a mischievous smile, 'Okay, are you ready?' before throwing me high into the air as I somersaulted into the deep end. The fun, the joy, the love for my dad. 'Again, again, again!' I shrieked, splashing my way back to his strong arms for more.

The phone rang, snapping me out of the daze. It was my sister's number. I hadn't been able to call my brother or sister for weeks. Isolation was easier than facing the people I hurt; autopilot kicked in again. I had to get the call over with to stop her turning up at the house.

'Hello,' I quavered.

'Hi, how are you doing?' she said. I could hear her sucking hard on a cigarette.

'I don't know really, not brilliant, I'm still signed off work.'

'Well, we want something back from you. You've given us nothing, no explanation, no ideas about how to get yourself out of this hole you're in. No suggestions about how you can get yourself back on track, eh?'

31

Her lips slipped off the end of the filter as she took another hard drag. 'I don't know what to say. I'm sorry, the doctor's given me some more beta-blockers but I'm not sure they're working.' Half-truth, not a bad effort.

'I know you've been drinking – you sound fucked!'

'I haven't had a drink all day,' I said, preferring not to mention the blackout.

'You can't string a sentence together. I'm not even going to ask about cocaine.' She paused, hoping for some kind of response. 'I've been talking to someone from a recovery charity; his name's Dave. I'll text you his number. I needed to talk to someone.'

'Okay,' I said.

Her voice got angrier. 'Why don't you try and save your marriage? I know my brother is still in there somewhere!'

The first words of hope I'd heard for months. I was still in here somewhere, but where? I didn't know why I couldn't stop myself from ruining everything. I knew if I kept behaving the same way that eventually enough would be enough.

'Aaron, are you still there?'

'Yes, sorry, I'm just trying to think of something to say to you.'

'Stop telling me you're sorry.'

'Dave told me about a rehab in Cape Town. I think you should call them, check it out. I'll pay for you to get out there. Just do something!' Her voice peaked, tight with emotion. She hung up.

Cocooned inside a mental asylum of which I was the mad architect. Comfortable for so long in my sick skin, but now the pain began to break through. I'd believed I was living a luxurious life, pulling the wool over everyone's eyes while I embarked on my own indulgent trip. Every wake-up call my mind and body tried to give me was so easily squashed by the power of craving. The more drugs I used, the more strength I needed to find my way back. I had nothing else to lose but the unseen force which kept my heart beating. And then, the pain I'd been secretly dreading, hoping it would be quick, hit my chest like a train. Its imprint would never leave me. The years of abuse finally caught up with my beating heart, with the intensity of a guillotine slicing my chest open. It held me in a vice so tight I couldn't even scream, but then a light tapping on the window made me flick my head anxiously, expecting to see an accusing human finger poking blame at me. Crow stood on the window ledge, tapping his beak against the glass. The pain suddenly disappeared. As we caught each other's gaze he started to hop excitedly along the length of the window, stopping momentarily to see if he still had my attention before continuing with his little jaunt.

I recalled all the other times I'd heard the familiar tip-tapping of his feet and beak. My dad had made a window extension on one side of the house through the slanting roof, so that the head of my bed fit snugly into the new alcove, a flat roof directly above my head. My binges prompted a strange tapping on the thin roof above me.

Sometimes this distracted me from my deeds, making me think that police were on the roof, prompting me to repeatedly twitch the curtains. It was the last sound I heard before losing consciousness and the first I heard when waking.

Tip-tap-tapping, tip-tap-tapping.

There my black feathered companion stayed, making at least twenty runs back and forth on the window ledge until suddenly he stopped and looked at me. I felt hypnotised; I couldn't blink. My eyelids would not respond to my brain. The glass lost its reflection. Crow launched his powerful engine-revving 'Cawwww!', hitting me like a tsunami ramming into land. A flash of light filled the room. I stared into the trashed bedroom, my crooked body sitting on the single bed. Head in hands, skin barely clinging to a skeletal frame, shadows of doom surrounding me. I wanted to scream at my body to run from the house, but I had no voice: run from the shadows out into the street and run, don't look back!

With that last thought the vision ended. I shuddered back into my body, the flight of freedom over as quickly as it started. I looked for Crow and caught a glimpse of his black silhouette from the corner of my eyes before his tail feathers vanished. A complete breakdown felt imminent. My heart pounded. The rattling metal of my dad's front door key freaked me out. My parents returned to find the outside walls of their house the only familiarity remaining. Mum screamed as she stepped on the pile of snails outside the front door, but that was only the beginning. Every room was blemished by my debauched behaviour. I twitched and scratched at my skin, muttering something about being in trouble and telling them about my sister's suggestion to go to Cape Town. My eyes darted around the walls, unable to look either of them in the eye. No one needed convincing, least of all me. I was tired of this life, bored of myself. I had nothing left to give. Game over. The next two days blurred by.

I eavesdropped on Mum's telephone calls with a doctor in Cape Town. My dad offered words of support.

'Aaron, does Karen know you're ill?' he asked.

A very good question: his insight was astounding as I had no idea what was happening.

I stayed in the house until the morning of my flight to Cape Town, a part of the world I'd never visited before. My daytime drinking had reduced to a half-pint nightcap of whisky to quell my nerves. Brief bursts of craving tried to persuade me to mug someone at a cash machine to pay for a final cocaine binge. I packed for what I thought would be a five-week trip. Not having checked myself into a rehab before, I had no idea what to prepare myself for.

My dad drove me away from Mum's melancholic wave, as I left for a city six thousand miles away. A city with which all I had to relate to was apartheid, great white shark cage diving, and Table Mountain, which always held my fascination. School geography lessons were etched in my mind with the teacher pointing at slides of this extraordinary piece of rock. It made a statement of grandeur for every other wonder of the world to take note of.

The journey to Heathrow with my dad was almost uneventful: just the token question, asking if someone was meeting me at Cape Town airport. He was as shell-shocked as I was. I stared through the faint reflection of my face in the car window, quietly relishing my last beer, soon to be consumed at the airport bar.

'Caw!' Crow flew next to the car, weaving in and out of telegraph poles and road signs. Darting ahead, he rested on top of a lamp post and as his feet settled – the light turned on.

As we passed his illuminated perch he flew ahead again, landing on a second lamp post – and the light turned on again.

I checked the other lamp posts in the road as we drove on; none of them was lit, and at five p.m. the remaining daylight didn't warrant any use of the street lighting. I lost sight of Crow after the second light. We crossed the River Thames at Richmond Bridge. Halfway across Crow burst up from the left side of the bridge and flew ahead of the car to the first lamp post at the end of the bridge. He landed on the metal lid of the lamp; nothing happened, and the car drew nearer. I opened my window, resting my head against the car door as we turned a slow right corner. I watched him intently. The wind cooled my face, the sun caught my eyes. Crow sounded his claxon again – and the light turned on.

Dad was gone in a handshake. I walked away wishing I

had the strength to open up and talk to him. My feelings were a mess. I shuffled through the check-in procedure, cleared security and quickly found the bar. I allowed myself one last drink to say goodbye to alcohol. We had to part. In all its wonderful colours and flavours, alcohol was my favourite drug; I'd been happily seduced. The end of the love affair was nigh.

Whatever the reasons for my slow attempted suicide, I didn't really give a shit. I didn't give a shit about anything but one thing: my last drink. I was going to say goodbye to alcohol with a cold pint of beer. The whole check-in procedure had been a blur, but I never forgot that last beer. It tasted so damn good. I sipped the snow-capped golden syrup as the cold bubbles fizzed against my lips. It took me half an hour to finish a drink which would have been gone in ten seconds a few days ago.

I texted the few remaining people I thought I could still call friends. Some returned brief replies wishing me luck, which was all I could expect from people I'd distanced myself from. I needed all the luck I could get. Unable to fit the word 'no' into my vocabulary when the flight attendant walked by, two more whisky and gingers graced my gullet on the ten-hour flight in the hope they'd send me off to la la land, which they did. My mind drifted from the window seat as I watched England fall away behind me.

I'd been disenchanted with my job as a social worker from the first day I sat down at a desk and turned on a computer. My heart sank as I wondered what the hell I'd done. I felt trapped in an office environment where forms, timescales and budgets were the staple diet of its employees. I instantly felt out of my comfort zone, missing the profoundly disabled children I used to work with every day. Of all the lessons I'd learnt in life, those children taught me the most powerful principles of humility and gratitude. How diminished I was now. My five-year tennis coaching career which had helped me get started with disabled children seemed so far away. I'd started coaching kids when I was twenty and although the marijuana eventually sapped my enthusiasm, I remember feeling so proud of myself for the way I helped sixteen tearaway kids from council estates have fun on cold Sunday mornings.

I thought about my black winged supernatural friend and how he'd kept me company as I took the elevator to hell. It was only in his absence that I realised he had been a companion to me. I missed his unpredictable appearances.

A cabin-crew announcement woke me with the news that it was a clear sunny day, pushing eighty-five degrees. I winced as I stepped off the plane into a wall of heat. I trod down the exit stairs gingerly; I'd been cocooned for so long in my depraved world that the elements hit me as if I were coming out of hibernation.

The visa officer looked up from my passport photo and gave me the obligatory three-second-stare, checking my face's resemblance to the version he had in his hand. It was a close call. The photo in his hand was over five years old. Fuller faced, sixty pounds heavier and with a decent head of hair before male patterned baldness took hold.

'What's the purpose of your visit?' he said.

'Medical treatment,' I said.

He paused, pursed his lips and reached for his stamp.

'Good luck with your treatment,' he said, handing me back the passport.

I walked on, my bottom lip quivering from the sentiment of a stranger who'd probably seen his fair share of addicts pass through the airport. I didn't have a clue what I was getting myself into. Rehab was not supposed to be on my curriculum vitae. As the taxi moved away I realised this was my only chance; I only had the strength to do this once and rehab hadn't even started. I'd come to the end of the line. All change please.

THREE

'This your first trip to Cape Town?' The driver tried to make polite conversation. It didn't take him long to figure out he was wasting his time. I'd lost the skill of talking with no props to loosen my tongue. I didn't know how long the car journey would take and I didn't care; however unfamiliar Cape Town was to me, it felt good to be surrounded by a new landscape with unfamiliar road signs, different traffic lights and trees I'd never seen before. I felt lighter as relief continued to take me thousands of miles away from the bombsite. The committee meeting in my head had adjourned. No drug dealer to call, no whisky to drink, and for the first time I didn't want either; it was the weirdest feeling. The world blurred by. My gaze relaxed onto the low sloping hills interrupted by the rust-coloured corrugated roofs of a township, meshing its people together. I opened the window and closed my eyes, resting, head on forearm. My blunted senses savoured the African sunshine as it warmed my broken skin. A gust of wind flowed through the window, filling the taxi, hugging my body as I drifted. The breeze soothed me with its whispering touch, telling me I was near to safety, asking me to let go of the old so a new life could find me.

The clattering wheels of a train woke me. The taxi had stopped at a level crossing. People were waiting for the barriers to lift with the passing of the last carriage. We were near the rehab in a residential area of mostly single-storey iron-gated houses. Razor-wire lined the tops of the walls. The ADT security company seemed to be a very popular choice; nearly every house displayed its 'Armed Response' metal plaque by the front gate. A hundred yards later the taxi arrived at a huge three-storey house used for the psychiatric unit. A giant grey tree stood in front of the house; the thick iron barred gate, flanked by a security post, slid open after a nod of recognition from the guard. I passed a sign on the gate posts which read 'Cedar Ridge Clinic, Restoring Lives' – no nerves or adrenalin bursting through my veins, no startled butterflies waking in my stomach. The gate closed behind me, guiding the car into a forecourt of a two-storey modern building. The driver got my bags out. Did I have to pay him? I had no cash. The rehab said they'd send a car, but not whether they would pay for it. My heart started to race, my breathing froze. I didn't know how to ask him if he needed paying – a situation usually easily dealt with scared the shit out of me, but it resolved itself when the driver set down my suitcase with an 'Okay.' I couldn't even manage to say 'Thank you' before he'd got back in his car and driven off.

The path leading to the office was flanked by bushes on one side and a fish pond on the other. A fountain played the random tunes of sprinkling water, lulling me into a brief moment of wishing I were entering a hotel. A spectacled woman in her fifties with tightly curled silver hair greeted me at the front door.

'Aaron Blake?' she said. Her perfect teeth shone as white as snow against her light brown complexion.

I offered a weak smile of acknowledgement on hearing my name spoken in a strong South African accent for the first time.

'I'm Elizabeth, the admissions nurse. How was your journey?'

'Not bad, thanks.' It was the second longest sentence I'd managed to string together in the last forty-eight hours.

'Please come into the office, we need to go through some forms. I have to search your luggage, just to make sure it's clear of drugs, alcohol, fictional books and music. It's all about focusing on the programme here, no distractions.'

'Okay, sure.' My heart raced with paranoia. What kind of programme did they have in store for me? I remembered the time my mother returned from Croatia to find she'd travelled there and back with an eighth of potent skunk weed in the side pocket of her case, left there by yours truly after I borrowed her luggage for a weekend away.

Elizabeth was slow and thorough with her search, using the time to find out more about me.

'Do you have any children?'

'No, we were thinking of trying but…' I hesitated, only wanting to say that everything was fucked up. 'Things aren't working out very well at the moment.' I rescued myself with a huge understatement.

'How about brothers and sisters?' she said, opening my wash bag.

'Yeah, I've got a sister and a brother, all older.' I remembered my last phone conversation with my sister before I'd left England. She answered the phone unable to talk, sobbing her eyes out.

'I'm so worried about you!' she finally managed to say. The clanking of whisky bottles in my pockets was ringing in her ears from the last time we'd met at my parents' house.

'I'm okay, don't worry about me.' But I wasn't okay and I was worried about myself.

Elizabeth stopped her search to hold up a small bottle of mouthwash. 'We'll have to keep this, there's alcohol in it.'

I hadn't missed the opportunity when I'd presumed the house was empty of alcohol; I hadn't felt remorse or regret for years. Elizabeth held eye contact with me, her gaze tinged with suspicion as she put the mouthwash to one side. I knew she thought I was lying; most people who walked through the doors of rehab hadn't told the truth for years.

'How much did you drink on the plane?' she asked.

'Two Jack Daniels and Coke,' I said.

'Is that all?'

'Yeah, I had a beer before I got on the plane, too.'

'Most people use their journey here to get as drunk and high as possible,' she said.

'Oh, no, I've had enough of all that now,' I said, struck by how quiet my conscience was, but Elizabeth looked at me as though she'd heard that a million times before. She finished searching my case, sliding her hand through a full-length inside pocket to make one last search. Her hand stopped halfway and picked out a white pill; she examined it closely.

'What's this?'

'Melatonin.' It was the first thing that came into my head and I hoped I was right. Melatonin was one of several sleep aids I had been using to help bring me down from cocaine, but I'd also been using ecstasy pills. Close to fifteen of them during a muddy Glastonbury binge. I'd left part of my soul behind in the farmer's field as I tried to drag my sorry arse through clay mud, and going by my mother's escape from a bizarre 'Midnight Express' encounter, the pill could've been anything.

'I'll have this tested,' she said, putting the pill to one side. 'We're almost done here, this form needs your signature. Please read it before you decide to sign and leave me with your wallet, passport and mobile phone; then I'll show you to your room. You'll get your mobile back when you leave. You can use the pay phone here after you've been here for five nights, between five and eight in the evening.'

I frowned as she reeled off more rules. I'd booked a return flight in five weeks. My manager Frank had granted me another six weeks sick leave, so I thought five weeks would be enough time to sort myself out, but all he knew was that I'd come here to see non-existent cousins. I gave Elizabeth my belongings. She watched my left hand as I drew it away.

'What happened to your hand?' she said.

I didn't know what she meant. I thought my hands were fine until I looked down at my palms. The skin was peppered with cigarette burns and frayed scabbing skin.

'I don't know,' was all I could muster, fearing the counsellors would add another defect to my name and cart me over to the psych unit, but I knew she knew. I felt the first thawing of my emotions; embarrassed and saddened at the sight of the self-inflicted damage, the guilty party was an impostor trying to tear me apart.

'Your one-to-one counsellor will agree on a weekly budget with you. You'll meet her tomorrow. It's normal protocol for new patients to detox with a three-day medication programme. Come back and see me at seven this evening.' She closed my case and showed me to my room, which was a large rectangular shape with four single beds, three in a row and one against the window. I hadn't shared a bedroom since my tennis coaching days in Philadelphia. Memories of the Indian guy nicknamed 'chocolate lip smacker' returned to haunt me, an apt alias for the aroused manner in which he woke himself each morning. A sudden longing for my bedroom in England came over me, but my nervous system, shot to pieces, stopped me from concentrating on anything for more than a few seconds. The longing faded into tiredness brought on at the sight of a bed. I thanked Elizabeth with my last reserves of energy, laid my head on the pillow, and drifted into dreamless sleep with my first breath. One journey ended; another had just begun.

I woke confused by my surroundings with a deep rhythmic hum filling my head. Boom boom boom! It was deafening, like King Kong was on his way. I shook my head from side to side, hitting the heel of my hand against the side of my head to release whatever was causing the noise, and then the breakfast soundtrack of murmuring voices and the clinking of cutlery hummed up from downstairs. Sunshine streamed through a gap in the curtains, telling me I'd slept through my first night fully clothed with a blanket pulled over me by a nurse. Probably Elizabeth, arriving to give me my first detox pill, which I vaguely remembered taking. One of the other beds had been slept in; it seemed that its occupant had dragged the bed sheets half off in some kind of mad rush to leave the room. I drank in the array of greens and yellows from the tall garden outside my room as the sunshine and wind mixed a beautiful palate of colours, painting me a beautiful morning picture.

Then I caught sight of a crow over my shoulder on a branch at my level, just watching, waiting. His presence held me still. I tried moving, but my muscles didn't respond. I closed my eyes to hide from a glimpse of my reflection in the window when the wind hurled itself at me through the windows, forcing them open so hard that the hinges creaked with the strain. Then the sound I hadn't heard since England screwed into my head like a bizarre form of Chinese water torture. A pigeon found me with heat-seeking precision. It stood on the roof above my window, cooing its evil mantra.

'You promised her, you fucking promised her, Aaron!' It screamed.

I threw myself on the bed and slammed my head under the pillow to block out the noise, but the sounds twisted into my head. The pigeon was too close for the sound to be blocked out with a pillow. No music to distract me, and no way to explain to anyone what was happening for fear of being sent to the funny-farm. Maybe that was the best place for me.

Anger rose in my chest as I wished instant nasty termination on the plump grey bird. I had a violent vision of the pigeon being interrupted mid-coo by a shotgun. Psychosis had left me with morbid flashes. Car crashes, murders, strangers having sudden heart attacks, dying at my feet. My imagination was more vivid than I remembered before hitting rock bottom. I was about to have my wish granted. I leaned out the window to pull it shut.

The pigeon's babble grew louder – 'You fucking promised her!' – I fell from the bed to my knees, looking through the window to the crow as it spread its long black wings and launched from the branch; the pigeon stopped its assault, making its escape into the garden. The crow flew below the pigeon, forcing it back up, and then darted above, left and right, hemming the pigeon in from all directions. The pigeon was corralled straight back in my direction, aiming for me with one last kamikaze run. I tugged the window shut moments before it slammed into the glass. An imprint of its flung-open wings and a spit of blood smudged the glass. Its broken neck sent it to the ground. The crow pulled away seconds before impact to return to the branch where it sat, in silence, facing me. I looked down to see who the woman was, shrieking and flapping her arms around her head to remove the scent of the dead pigeon. The area below my window opened from the canteen to the busy smoking area of the garden. The dead pigeon had cursed another client. It was not the best omen. I looked up at the crow. He was big, with a head as big as a tennis ball. All too familiar.

Suddenly he left the window ledge, returning seconds later with a fleeting landing just long enough to carefully place a snail on the ledge before he left again. He returned with another snail, and gently placed it next to the first, before leaving with an excited 'Caw!' into the air. This continued until the ledge was so crowded with snails they cascaded onto the ground. A nurse came out in the process of lighting a cigarette, oblivious to the crunching shells under her feet, instantly reminding me of my mother's screech as she did the same thing.

The crow's caws got louder as he embarked on a new mission, this time dropping small stones mid-flight as he flew towards my window, pulling up at the last minute, just late enough to hear his payload ping against the window. His cawing increasing in volume with each ping of the window. I knew nothing about the migratory habits of crows or any birds for that matter, but even with my ignorance I was never going to entertain the possibility that a crow had followed me to Cape Town. The idea was preposterous and, even if I did believe it, telling anyone at rehab about such an outlandish thing would have brought heavier persuasion to continue with more than one month of treatment. Nothing was going to stop me getting on that plane in five weeks. That was all I needed to detox.

The crow came back to rest on the ledge again. He stopped still and gave a frustrated hop in the air. He flew away again, circling the gardens, gliding in smooth swoops between the trees and bushes, momentarily resting on the back of a bench to see if I was still looking. Satisfied he had his audience, he made another circuit flying in ever-decreasing circles over the top of a garden lamp. His feathers momentarily camouflaged him as he skimmed close to the ground. The tall black metal pole was capped with a large white ball lampshade. He flapped his wings once, making a beautiful vertical line with the black pole, his body pausing feet above the lamp. He hovered. Time suspended him for just long enough to spread his wings to full span before he parachuted gracefully onto the lamp. His black-clawed feet touched the curved white frosted glass and the light – turned on.

He arrived on the window ledge next to my bed, feet

facing me, and cocked his head to one side quizzically.

'Aren't you going to say hello then? A thank you would be nice. Those pigeons aren't going to give up that easily,' Crow said.

'It can't be yo… you can't have flown all the way out here!' But then something he'd said struck me. 'So you can hear it too? The pigeons shouting at me?'

'You still haven't got it, have you?' he said, cocking his head to the other side.

I sat in stunned silence for a minute. 'No, you're gonna have to tell me,' I said, finally able to acknowledge the fact that Crow had found me again.

'No I'm not, you'll have to figure it out yourself. That's why you're here – well, partly. If it weren't for me your parents would've found your corpse before you got on the plane.' He did a celebratory jig on the window ledge. Tip-tap-tapping, tip-tap-tapping.

'That was you!?' I said, alarmed as I remembered the insanity in England.

'Yours truly.' Crow stopped his jig and moonwalked across the window ledge. 'I've been with you for longer than you know, Aaron.' The Cape Doctor wind, known for its smog-cleansing power, came into town for its afternoon rounds, cooling sweaty brows, inducing siestas. 'Mmmm, I love that wind. You chose a good country for rehab, Aaron; the Doctor can blow for weeks. You have no idea how much fun it is to fly in a wind like that.'

'Where have you come from, Crow?' I said, shuffling towards the window to be closer to his impressive silky blackness.

'I've come from the darkness, Aaron, from the same place you've come from… the edge. The thing is you've been quite determined to take yourself to the edge ever since you were a baby. I've had my work cut out for me, bringing you back all those times,' he said, before extracting a snail from its shell and swallowing it.

'You'll have to expand on that a little. I'm still coming to terms with this conversation. I'm not dreaming, am I?'

'What do you think? Or more importantly, what do you feel?'

I looked at my palms and picked a small slither of scab from the burns on each hand to find the pain, which was reassuring and at the same time strangely exciting.

'Okay, so I'm not dreaming. What times?' I said.

Crow hopped to within striking distance of my face; I could see sporadic sparks of light in his black eyes. 'I know where you got those scars under your chin, Aaron. I was there when you fell through that window as a one-year-old. It was no fluke that the glass missed your jugular. And eight years later I gave your sister the strength to fish you out from the bottom of that swimming pool. You always kept me on my toes, Aaron. When you were fifteen-years-old that firework rocket would've blinded you if I hadn't diverted it… you said I was not a friend of yours, but I've done more for you than most friends ever would! But I had to repay you somehow.'

My mouth hung open as I listened to Crow reel off the accidents which had nearly killed or maimed me. Brushing my fingers over the thick scar tissue under my chin, I could only imagine the shock my parents felt as they found my head poking through a window in the front door of our house after my eagerness to reach a toy had toppled over my baby-walker. I took pride in hearing that it took four nurses to hold me down while they stitched up my chin. I'd always wondered how close I'd come to slashing my throat. My second brush with death was imprinted much more clearly on my mind. The force of my so-called friend's hands pushing into my back never left me; I'd been at the bottom of the pool before I'd known what'd hit me. My flailing arms and legs did nothing to save me, but the heroic vision of my fifteen-year-old sister breaking the silver surface of the water, descending with the ease of an otter to retrieve her little brother, always took precedence over any fearful memories. My infatuation with fire bordered on being another addiction; nothing quelled my desire to get as close to it as possible. The stretched ribbon skin on the back of my right hand never let me forget the time a firework blew up in my face as I'd let it off in broad daylight. I'd always marvelled at how the blast missed my face but singed most of the hair from my head.

'Repay me for what?' I said.

Crow left the window ledge to fly a quick circuit of the garden, prompting startled birdcalls from the smaller members of his species as they nestled in their green havens. He returned to me, clearly taking delight in the stir he'd caused.

'You're not ready to know, Aaron. You need to focus on this place for a while. All in good time, all in good time.' He sipped another snail from its shell and was gone in a blink.

Addiction had wiped the slate clean and that was the whole idea: a wake-up call. In that empty rehab bedroom, something started to stir. I knew I needed help, that's why I'd come to Cape Town, to put my life in someone else's hands because mine were killing me. I'd run away from my responsibility as a husband; no one, including myself, really knew who the real me was anymore. There was very little left worth knowing, but there was something: a spark of light; a memory of living life in colour. Not dying in the grey stale air of a bedroom with the curtains closed. Now I was offered a choice, a no-brainer. The first step started here, one foot in front of the other, baby steps. Only one direction to follow: the destination wasn't important, just as long as the path was new.

FOUR

I was wondering who my roommate was when a tall, square-jawed, lanky guy with blonde hair neatly side-parted bounced to the door, clutching a large blue book under his arm. He couldn't stand still for more than a few seconds, pacing erratically around the room and then finally sitting down on his bed. He rested the blue book next to him, checking it obsessively several times before he clamped his hands tightly over his crossed elbows, locking in place like a tightly coiled spring.

'Morning, Aaron, I'm your roomy Jimmy. How's it, as they say?'

'It's hungry,' I said, feeling the first hunger pang for months as my stomach started waking up.

'Come and have some breakfast. I'll show you the ropes until you get the hang of things. What are you in for?' he said with a mischievous smile.

'What do you mean? It's not a prison, is it?'

He laughed. 'No, I mean what drugs were you using?'

I didn't feel like running off a whole list of every drug I'd tried, which included the contents of twenty cold-remedy capsules one barren afternoon. I gave him the two main culprits. 'Cocaine and alcohol. What about you?'

'Wine, cocaine, work, money, women… sometimes men, the whole caboodle. See you downstairs in a minute – come and get some breakfast.' Releasing his elbows, he sprang off the bed and out of the room like a Labrador puppy, without the joy. Five seconds later he sprinted back into the room looking as though he were about to have a panic attack.

'Shit, nearly forgot my Big Book!' He snatched up the Alcoholics Anonymous handbook from the bed. 'Acceptance is the answer to all my problems, fella, acceptance is the keeeeey!' His voice faded as he disappeared from view. I liked him instantly. Something about his honesty made me lower my guard a little, helping me settle in to the clinical atmosphere. And there was no danger of Jimmy's flighty personality making me feel claustrophobic, or so I thought.

I started to dress my wounded body; aches and pains surfaced from deep within my body. I was so accustomed to the physical injuries I sustained in blackout that I'd lost track of the total amount of damage. My first night of rest for a millennium started to release the pain; the anaesthetic was wearing off. I stared at my big toes, both of them crooked from multiple fractures, the left toe broken in three places. Running my fingers down the length of two of my ribs I found the jutting bones crookedly fused by the incessant cocaine edginess, never resting enough to give them a chance to heal. My nicotine-stained fingers and palms were peppered with cigarette burns and cuts from desperate lunges under furniture to find that elusive wrap of cocaine. I fumbled with my shoe laces with the dexterity of a five-year-old. I'd lost all familiarity with my basic self-care skills; pausing momentarily, I trawled my memory for the instructions on how to tie a shoe lace. I didn't know how to look anyone in the eye when I talked to them. I'd forgotten how to laugh, my sense of humour deserted me. If someone asked me what my favourite colour was, I'd say I didn't know… I didn't know who I used to be… who I was… or who I wanted to be. I had to start retracing my steps to make sense of this tangled mess, and to do that I needed fuel.

'Thank God!' Jimmy said as I sat down releasing a huge sigh.

'What's up?' I said, pulling my seat forward with food completely hiding the surface area of my plate.

'I have to sit at the table for five minutes after I've finished my food, counsellors' orders. Since I arrived last week and started my detox I can't sit in a chair for more than a few minutes. I can't stand still without twitching. My nervous system doesn't know which way to turn. I feel like a live cat's been dropped inside me and it's trying to claw its way out. They say it'll pass, or 'this too shall pass', or something like that: always preaching from the Big Book.' Jimmy held his elbows tightly, rocking back and forth.

'What are p and d's?' I said, looking at the timetable on the wall.

'Powerlessness and damages, it's basically what the twenty-eight-day programme is. We get split into groups with one or two counsellors and we take it in turns to talk about how drugs fucked us and our families up. It can be brutal, like psychological Russian roulette. You'll see a counsellor bring in a piece of paper and put it on the floor next to them, and everyone starts wondering if it's for them. Cassie got shot yesterday.'

Jimmy nodded over my shoulder to the next table where a girl in her early twenties sat with her head in her hands. Her face was hidden by her forearms which were latticed with scars and partly healed sets of lacerated tally lines cut into her skin. I was familiar with my own form of self-harm, but I'd never seen such self-mutilation. I counted four complete sets of tallies, twenty cuts, before she dropped her arms and lifted her head, prompted by Jimmy's reference to her troubles. She had cropped tomboy red hair and a cute button nose bridged with freckles which spread to her cheeks and tumbled onto her shoulders, exposed by a tight-fitting white vest. Her already piercing ice-blue eyes were intensified by a glassy film of tears. I was mesmerised.

'See you upstairs for round two, guys. No rest for the wicked.' Cassie forced a smile and stood up, scraping the chair with the back of her legs. The sound shocked me away from exploring her body.

Jimmy sprang up like a jack-in-the-box. 'That's my five

minutes – come upstairs when you're done. They lock the doors bang on time to keep out late arrivals. Best not be late, fail to plan, plan to fail!' He hollered another recovery slogan at me, waving the Big Book in the air as he bounced away. He was learning fast. I hadn't even had my first lesson and I was already distracted.

I took my place in an upstairs room outside the nurses' station. I was entering unknown territory with strangers. Jimmy and Cassie sat on either side of me, their proximity and prior knowledge of what was about to unfold providing a strange mix of reassurance and anxiety. They recognized the need to stick together. An elderly gentleman with a large belly and a full head of silver hair sat opposite me, smiling nervously. There were two empty chairs ready for the counsellors. A man and woman entered on cue with blank expressions, pen and paper in hand. The man wore a checked collared shirt and gold-rimmed glasses. His shiny leather shoes poked from perfectly creased trousers. His stern expression and meticulous presentation reminded me of my first head teacher, notorious for caning pupils, namely yours truly, for offences as slight as sniggering at his flies being undone as we passed him in the corridor.

'Good morning, Aaron, I'm Mark, this is Lucy. As this is your first session we suggest you listen to start with and perhaps join in later when you're ready.'

Lucy's reputation preceded her. Eavesdropped conversations in the dining room talked about her as the 'Pit-bull': an alias that must've described her personality as it didn't fit her pristine milky complexion indented with brown eyes, perfectly framed by long straight chocolate hair. Her face was the crowning glory of a body which formed the perfect package and I wanted to unwrap it. Stirrings of carnal desires for other women without the boost of chemicals were shaking me like the sudden onset of airplane turbulence. The expression of her mouth was an unsolvable riddle, the hint of a Mona Lisa smile so easily switched to someone looking very pissed off and not to be fucked with; it just made her more intriguing. The wood growing in my shorts was chopped down by the abrupt shutting of the door. The turning of the key sealed our fate for the next hour. We sat in sober silence, an open invitation for someone to paint a story of sadness and insanity on the canvas of the quiet room.

Five minutes passed; the air in the room was thick with defiance. Jimmy squirmed on his chair, either about to wet himself or hit the ceiling. Cassie sat at a disinterested angle, staring out of the window in a daydream trance, miles away. Just when it looked as if she was deflating to the point of slipping off her chair she started humming the melody to Radiohead's 'You Do It To Yourself', with a ventriloquist's skill. Her fingers moved along an air guitar's fret board. I did a double-take, making sure it really was her and not a new skill the pigeon had learnt.

'As you seem the most vocal today, you can start, Cassie,' Lucy said, her accent instantly giving away English roots.

'And that's what really hurts…' Cassie's humming

turned into song. 'What do you think I could possibly have to say? They're the ones addicted to drugs. He's more fucked up than I am.' She nodded in my direction.

'Why do you think you're here?' Mark said.

'Because Mum and Dad said so; everything's because they say so.'

'Your parents have given us some clues. This is from them,' Lucy said, unfolding a piece of paper in true Pitbull style.

'No shit!' Cassie thumped her legs.

'This is written by your dad,' Lucy continued. 'We started to notice missing kitchen knives and scissors when Cassie was fifteen. She spent more time in her room, refusing to come down for meals and wearing long sleeves in the hottest weather. We'd been talking about her exam results one day; she had to stay back a year for several retakes. She stormed off to her room, which was above the lounge. Soon afterwards I heard a thud upstairs. I found her topless. She'd cut crosses into her forearms, one for each failed exam.'

'He's so false,' Cassie interrupted, desperate to defend herself. 'We had a shouting match and I won. Mum and Dad can't accept I'm not as smart as my brother and won't be joining him as a business apprentice in the city. All that cash they spent on my extra tuition did nothing; now they have to spend more on my psychotherapy. Serves them right. I pleaded with them to send me to music college, but they wouldn't listen. I'd sit in my bedroom writing and playing my songs all day, praying I'd hear one of them come up and knock on my door to say how much they liked my music, but they ignored me like they always do. Dad said I'd never make anything of myself playing guitar and he stopped paying for my lessons. I got him back though, didn't I…? Bastard!'

'How?' Lucy said

Cassie realised she'd said too much. Lucy had found the button. Cassie hid her face with her white knuckled fists tightly gripping the short fringe of her thick red hair.

'You know you've lost control, Cassie. Can't you see? You cut to take some control back from your parents, but you went too far, and it's controlling you now.' Lucy let Cassie's emotion surge up, finally released from the vaults of her fractured heart, every piece of scar tissue weighted with emotions she couldn't express with words.

Cassie's sobbing started slowly. Little peeps of sound seeped from her grimacing lips. She squirmed into a foetal position and buried her head in the crook of her elbow. Her body shuddered, and she tried to catch her breath as the pain surfaced. Lucy put down the piece of written touch-paper, the fire lit, no more reading required. I felt my social work training kick in, instinctively wanting to console and sympathise with Cassie's predicament.

'It's okay, Cassie,' I said. 'Your parents obviously can't see what kind of pressure they're putting on you. Let it out.'

Oblivious to the strict unspoken rules of these sessions, I'd pulled the trigger for Mark to make his own assault on me. I wasn't there to adopt any kind of professional role, and he was about to remind me of the real reason I was sitting in that room. His body tightened, sensing the bait he was about to catch.

'So you think you're an expert do you, Aaron? How does it feel that your wife is divorcing you because you couldn't stop drinking? You couldn't give a shit about how she felt. You just got yourself high as a kite night after night. Do you really think she's going to want you back now? You've lost your marriage, Aaron; look where you are. You've so fucked it up!'

His words hit me like a battering ram, assaulting me with every syllable slung with his sharp South African tongue. His swearing surprised me, and it was supposed to. Gone was the illusion that the counsellors would adopt a softly-softly approach. I'd only ever accused myself of hurting Karen in the safe silence of my thoughts. No one had ever echoed the thoughts I had as I careered out of control down the slippery slope from social worker to junkie. One thought got louder and louder as I scored more and more cocaine. If I couldn't stop I knew she was going to divorce me; she'd have no choice. Full credit to Mark: he'd got the bulls-eye.

'How does that make you feel, Aaron?' He wanted an answer.

'Like shit,' I said.

I hadn't cried for years. I'd been so happy dragging myself down to rock-bottom. No one grabbed me by the scruff of the neck and told me to sort it out. I wouldn't have listened anyway. There was always more nice warm shit to sink into.

I had stashed away a lot of pain inside the empty recesses of my heart. Deep inside my mind, body and soul, the guilt and remorse lay encased in the bedrock of my bones. Mark had made the first cracks. I felt them spread like an earthquake opening the seabed, stirring the heavy sea of denial lying above. A tsunami shock-wave of emotion gathered itself, throwing itself headlong into me. My heart felt the impact as years of feelings poured out of their skeletal tombs into my arteries, bottlenecking into my capillaries, competing to see which one would be the first to make me feel something, anything! They all hit me at once. Goosebumps stood my hairs on end as tears broke through, but there was something else I didn't expect. The tears felt good, so new; they soothed me. It felt safe to let them flow into the river of emotion carving out this new direction. At that moment I surrendered. I cried tears of hurt that felt so good because I could set them free from where they had lain inside, festering away at my spirit.

'You know you have a disease don't you, Aaron?' Mark said.

'What do you mean?'

'Addiction is an illness, a disease. There's no reason to feel guilty,' he said.

I looked at him through blurred eyes. His words made sense to me as the relief spread and my shoulders dropped their tension momentarily. But I wasn't ready to accept his explanation. It was too soon to let myself off the hook. So much easier to keep the spirit sick with a guilty malady;

surely no disease could make me sink so low?

'I'm struggling with that idea,' I said.

'Because it's easier to feel guilty?' he said.

He was right. The junkie on my back wasn't ready to take his claws out. He clung on grinning wide, enjoying the ride he'd been on for far too long to just hop off and go without a proper farewell. The tears flowed. Cleansing, purifying. It was getting slippery for the junkie on my back. He was losing his grip.

The session ended unceremoniously. Mark and Lucy just stood up without so much as a 'goodbye' and left the room in quiet satisfaction that something had given. All they wanted to see were chinks in our armour of denial, something to pry open a crack that would let the stale air out and replace it with nectar of fresh light. They did their job well; a claw retracted from my shoulder.

This was time to embrace change. Something started to happen: a process worked from within, churning up the shit and sludge I took so much pleasure wallowing in. Whether it was my perception which was changing or something more powerful cleansing the marks of abuse, I didn't know or bother to question. One thing stayed with me during the early days of treatment; things had got as bad as they needed to. I wasn't going back to the edge, but I couldn't remember what happiness felt like. Could I remember who I was? Could I make it? I didn't even know what the word sobriety meant until I got to Cape Town.

I took a detour on the way back to my room to a small balcony overlooking the car park, where I stood at eye-level with the tall lush vegetation. The balcony was no bigger than a priest's pulpit. Crow perched on a swaying palm branch, twitching his tail feathers to keep his balance. He wasn't watching me; he was much more interested in the car park, waiting until Mark left the building with his briefcase and jangling car keys. Crow took flight, making a beeline for him just as he got to his car, perfectly shooting his shitty payload on the back of Mark's head. Mark screamed in disgust as his hand explored and found the excrement on his head. He looked up to find the culprit as Crow swooped from the roof behind me to leave a second shit-bomb smack bang in the middle of Mark's face: his spectacles were covered in whitewash. Realising he was under attack and shielding his face with his elbow, Mark fumbled his way into the car moments before the black bird made its largest deposit, thumping on the car door. The trees erupted with the noise of crows cawing with delight as Mark's car made a tyre-screeching escape from the car park.

I looked at the empty sky, scouring the trees, but they were gone, mission accomplished, or maybe they had fled from the wind beginning to rise. I heard it long before I felt its tentative first touch on my skin, searching for me. I gripped the balcony rail tighter. Perturbed by the rumble surging through the suburban jungle, plants danced wildly as the invisible force gathered pace like a tube-train approaching from the darkness of a tunnel. An announcement warning it wasn't stopping at the next station would have helped me to brace myself as the impact caught me head-on. The balcony doors slammed shut, enclosing me on the small parapet. I gripped the rail tightly as the wind flung me off balance. My ears rushed with the rage of nature as the infamous South Eastern wind gave me a dose of its medicine. It blew through me with a biblical force; I white-knuckled it through the solo rollercoaster ride, shutting my eyes against the bludgeoning. This was no attack, though. My knees buckled as I heard the wind suck itself away. I saved myself from hitting the concrete with my hands which tingled with energy, and as it flowed through me on the balcony, pages of my past opened again.

My hands trembled with apprehension as I waited to read the memories. I'd always felt different. I remembered one of my team leaders telling me, 'You're a space cadet, Aaron, but space cadets are some of my favourite kinds of people.' Recurring childhood nightmares haunted me into my early teenage years, but these were no normal nightmares. They came to me when I was wide awake, sensing a spectral presence observing me. I frequently screamed the house down until someone came to reassure me. As I moved into my teenage years the menace changed with the different houses we lived in. Phantom breathing kept me company in the darkened corner of my bedroom.

During the day I lived with a heightened sensitivity to everything. Other people's expressions transmitted exactly what they were feeling. Walking through crowds was an overwhelming sensory experience which turned Waterloo Station's concourse into a dreadful obstacle course, making me walk close to the side walls until I reached the safety of the platform. Changes in the weather distracted me from whatever I was supposed to be doing as if my body was being molecularly altered by the forces of nature. Occasionally I heard people's thoughts before they spoke them. Unnerved by innate knowledge that I was psychic and with no one to confide in, I could hear the universe trying to tell me about my gifts. It nudged me from within, but other internal voices tinged with failure and disappointment told me I was a substandard human being, that no such gifts had been bestowed on me and the last thing in the world I could be was important.

I honed my psychic skills at personal development classes at the Spiritualist Association of Great Britain in Belgrave Square. My journeys to and from the centre of London were mini adventures. I never knew what was going to happen during the sessions, but whether it was with me or someone else, something wonderfully spooky always did.

The classes had an air of selectivity about them. A successful interview with the Vice President, Glynis Partridge, was a prerequisite before I could join the 'clairvoyant club'. Glynis was a small lady whose hunched posture and receding hairline of thin silver hair gave the impression of frailty, but this was belied by her gaze, her eyes rarely blinking as they looked a few inches above my head, probably at dancing pixies, only glancing at me to ask why I wanted to join the classes.

I told her about how I'd followed Mystic Mike's

guidance to explore Reiki, and about the initiation.

Margaret had sat me in a chair with my eyes closed and my hands in a praying clasp while she moved them up and down, left and right, blowing onto them and into my face. At one point she lowered her hands to a few inches above my head, channelled energy pressing down on my scalp. The pressure increased as a deep humming sound filled my head; it seemed to come from inside me and all around. I wanted to shout out in awe. As her hands touched my head the sound stopped and there was this silence, like the deepest cave. In that moment I had a feeling of connection like nothing on this earth; in the centre of the darkness behind my eyes a small white orb held still, growing brighter with every second. Margaret signalled the end of the attunement with a loud clap – it needed to be loud as I was quite happy, wherever I was. I opened my eyes and we exchanged smiles. I tried to get out of my chair. As I leant forward to stand up I hit an invisible wall of energy, pushing me back into my chair by force. I felt inclined to wait. I didn't know what to do. Margaret was smiling at me. I tried again and this time rose to my feet. I returned to my seat on the sofa and, ever so softly, my hands started tingling. At first I couldn't tell if it was just pins and needles from how I'd been sitting, but my circulation felt fine and a warm glow began to cover my fingers, spreading down to my wrists. The tingling accelerated gradually. I held my hands in front of my face, staring at them, speechless. During the day we practised treating others in the group and each time I laid my hands on someone the buzzing increased, accompanied by heat or a strange coldness, and then I'd lose all sense of having hands at all as the energy flowed like Niagara Falls from the cosmos, through me.

That night we had some friends over for dinner. I touched my wine glass in a gentle cheers with the woman next to me and the stem of the glass broke clean off. Her eyes welled up with tears; she was muted by a lump of emotion in her throat as my supercharged aura enveloped her. 'I could kiss your feet right now,' she said.

My vision was never the same after the initiation. When I relaxed I saw people shining; their auras were sometimes so bright I became distracted from the conversation. Plants appeared to move with not even the slightest of breezes present, as I picked up on their life force. But the biggest distraction came when I closed my eyes. Darkness had been replaced by sparkles of golden light, dancing with such brightness that they kept me awake at night. When I opened my eyes for relief the light got brighter in the bedroom. I didn't fear the random shapes and shadows which swam in the electric air. It felt different from the imposing presences summoned by my drug use. Another dimension opened right in front of my eyes, surrounding me. My childhood experiences took away any surprise at the revelation of the existence of cosmic forces. A few weeks after the initiation faces started to appear in the golden light behind my eyes whenever I closed them; they seemed to be asking me to notice them.

Glynis wasn't surprised at my story. She proudly

ushered me into the room used for group psychic platform readings, to show me the chair Arthur Conan Doyle had sat in to write his Sherlock Holmes books. As we walked into the room she paused, grabbing my arm. 'I don't give everyone this opportunity, you know.' Pulling back floor-to-ceiling red velvet curtains at the front of a room filled with chairs, she revealed an ornately carved mahogany chair with long arm rests and a high intricate grapevine back. Its sides were shaped with small church spires signifying the author's spirit worship. Glynis beckoned me to sit, and a force shot through my body as soon as my backside touched the seat. I wondered if she was mischievously shielding an electrical socket which powered the chair for her amusement. Shocked and embarrassed by my profanity I leapt out of the chair to see a smile of satisfaction on her face. I had passed the interview.

I was particularly good at two of the psychic exercises. Psychometry enabled me to receive information about people if I held a possession of theirs in my hands, and aura readings allowed me to send out energy from my solar plexus in a radar fashion to sense things about the other person. I saw how the cutest Japanese girl had spent her day soaking in a bubble bath, eating pears and listening to her vinyl collection. There's nothing more enticing than a bashful Japanese girl.

My greatest success came when I was chosen to demonstrate a reading with Glynis' bracelet. She decided, for the first and only time, to attend our session. She handed me her bracelet made of Jade beads, and I cupped it in both hands and closed my eyes.

'I can see a white cat,' I said. 'It has long hair... a big white cat.'

'Yes, I can take that, I hate white cats,' Glynis said.

Next came a gold pocket watch, floating into my mind; the Roman numeral clock face was partly hidden by the lid, and the chain dangled loose.

'I gave my husband a gold watch last week. It was our anniversary. Well done,' Glynis said.

My head stayed blank for a while before the next object appeared. 'There's a small black suitcase on a round mahogany table.' The energy inside my hands fizzed faster. 'I can see inside the case – there's a small stringed instrument, possibly a violin. And I can see a river flowing, there are lush green grass banks next to it... I feel like I'm in France.'

'Well, my nephew is touring with an orchestra at the moment, in France,' Glynis chuckled.

'Oh, gosh, what's this? A bandstand, I think. Yes, there's a bandstand in a park, but it's empty, there isn't a band playing.'

'Oh, how wonderful, yes, I love going to watch bands play in parks, but last week I went all the way to Eastbourne to see one and there was no one there. I was so disappointed,' Glynis said.

The energy subsided and I felt myself become more present in the room again. As the session ended I left quickly, surprised at myself; I felt as if I needed to escape with something precious I'd just found out about myself. I wondered what else I was capable of, but the lure of drugs and alcohol became harder to refuse. I wasn't completely sure where the explorations of my energy were going, I knew it was important to unlock my potential. But as the junkie's claws dug deeper into my back, I became cocky with my abilities. I remembered the last paranormal event before I lost touch with that other reality. I used the 'pick a card, any card' trick as everyone scraped the last morsels of Christmas pudding and brandy cream from their bowls. My cousin sat next to me keeping the card he chose out of sight, under his jumper. I closed my eyes and directed my attention towards him, seeing the King of Hearts in my mind's eye. His jaw dropped. He took the card out from under his jumper and laid it on the table, where it stayed for a few seconds before flying two feet across the table and sticking to the top of a lit candle. A knock on the balcony door rattled me out of my memories. Jimmy poked his head through tentatively.

'You okay, Aaron?' he said, slowly stepping onto the balcony. 'They gave you a rough time in there.'

'Not sure, I guess that's the name of the game, I've never had it told to me like that,' I said.

Jimmy stepped to the edge of the balcony and looked down over the edge.

'See that bush down there?' He pointed to a large spiky plant about two metres in diameter. 'That's where they found me on my first night here. I hid a bottle of vodka under it when I got out of the taxi. I drank all the way, had to get as much Pinot Grigio down me before I called last orders on my drinking. When I got here I couldn't bear the thought of giving up drinking so I had my last drink down there on my first night. Sure enough they found me and carried me back to my room, not because I was putting up a fight, I couldn't stand up. The counsellors told me I screamed all night for my children to come back to me. I've got twin seven-year-old girls. My wife has a restraining order on me and won't let me see them. This place is my last chance to see them again.'

'The divorce makes things pretty final. I knew if I kept using I'd lose her.' Tears began to rise out of the reservoir of subdued emotion Mark had helped me find, seeping out of the crack in my heart, broken not by Karen's reluctance to have me back but because now, without alcohol, I began to remember we'd been best friends, with never a harsh word spoken between us until addiction stuck its claws into me.

Jimmy could only look at me; no words came to comfort. He was still finding his feet and in rehab you can't sort out anyone else's shit for them.

'Come on, we've got another session after lunch, best get some food, you're gonna need it. They don't let up. I'll tell you about the life story work we have to do.'

'Life story work?' I said. Warning signs flashed up with dinging bells.

'Yep, we all have to write a two-thousand-word life story and share it with the group. It's supposed to help us put the pieces back together, or see where they fell apart, more like.' Jimmy chuckled.

'Shit, I wouldn't know where to start,' I said, scrambling for the jigsaw pieces of my life.

'Don't worry, they won't grade you. I only managed a thousand words; it's amazing how much I enjoyed the self-indulgence of it all.'

Jimmy put his hand on my shoulder as we walked to the canteen. I didn't recognise the feeling of physical reassurance and I wasn't sure I liked it. My muscles tightened away from his attempt to console me. Paranoia hit me again; his touch felt invasive. I wanted to pull away from him, but I had no idea how to assert myself; I hadn't an ounce of confidence left. Psychosis had physically and mentally torn me apart. I went from liking Jimmy to feeling violated by his dirty hand. The invisible prying hands that tugged me into a straitjacket, returned to me in the light of day. I wanted everyone to keep their distance, including Jimmy. Was he a heterosexual with good 'buddy' intentions? No idea. I was over-shadowed by homophobic paranoia, so I quickened my pace. The sooner we got to the canteen the better.

'I can barely remember the last month, let alone the last few years. I can only remember the times I hurt myself and….' The thought of playing with my father returned to me. There were roses among the thorns.

Jimmy removed his hand from my shoulder as we entered the canteen, prompting my silent sigh of relief before another memory flashed into my eyes.

'Oh God, not boerewors sausage again!' Jimmy said.

My hearing acted in self-defence, muting him out as

the flashback returned me to my wedding day, sitting alone on a garden bench outside the marquee. The happiest day of my life overwhelmed me. I needed respite from the weight of the occasion and that was the whole problem; I couldn't let myself feel the happiness and love flowing generously around me that day. I was scared of my self-destructive intentions and the depression slowly creeping over me, but I couldn't tell anyone, not even the guest who came to sit with me. I must've looked a strange sight, the groom on his own in his new mother-in-law's garden. And then I felt fear returning as I drew blank sheets. Emptiness wherever I grasped for meaning in my life. I felt dizzy, nothing made sense to me, the committee meeting in my head reconvened. The stream of drugs in my body thinned to a trickle, the supply almost cut off. Tears began to flow, carrying away the toxic waste clogging access to my soul's purity. My memories were a tangled ball of twine I had to unravel, but my nervous system was in shock. I had to retrieve more than just the random pieces of a jigsaw that had flown to me on the balcony. At least I thought they were random, but there was a method in the madness.

FIVE

Every week began and ended with a community meeting, designed to bring us closer together as a group. After breakfast on my first Monday at Cedar Ridge we all filtered into the lecture room and sat around the edges. It was the first time I'd seen everyone together. Twenty-four people with varying degrees of denial, but with one thing in common: powerlessness. The Twelve Steps of Alcoholics Anonymous adorned the wall to my left. I'd never seen them before and the mention of 'God' gave me the heebeegeebees, but I understood what the first one was telling me straight away. My life had become an unmanageable mess because of drugs and alcohol. The substances controlled me, diverting me from England to South Africa. I was in one of the most beautiful cities in the world, but unable to enjoy it as most people were. We were a mixed bag of colour and ages; addiction didn't discriminate. I felt exposed on my chair and had no clue what to do with my fidgeting hands so I sat on them, and stared at the floor trying to avoid the counsellors' attention. My attempt at invisibility was futile and just drew more attention.

'What's going on, Aaron? Look at you,' Mark said, standing in the centre of the room.

'I'm feeling homesick,' I said without thinking. I was surprised at myself for sharing something which made me feel even more vulnerable and when I thought about it, for the first time since my childhood, I missed Mum and Dad. I'd never been to boarding school, but I imagined it feeling very similar to how I felt at that exact moment.

'Who else can identify with how Aaron's feeling?' Mark turned around so that he could see the whole room. Everyone raised their hands, and I felt myself warming to the guy who'd pulverised me in my first group session. Mark sat down, the counsellors were mixed into the group; Lucy sat almost opposite him. Mark gave her a nod, tagging her to take centre floor.

'Some of you may remember hearing this when you arrived, if you were paying attention. It'll do no harm for you to hear it again. In fact it may save your life. Addiction is a progressive, terminal disease. If you decide to pick up again, you'll start off exactly where you finished before you walked – or were carried – through those doors.' Lucy stared at Jimmy, who was biting the cuticles from his fingers. 'I promise you,' she went on, 'if you're sitting in a rehab, drinking or using drugs will never be enjoyable again, no matter how hard you try to convince yourself. Your conscience won't let you forget you tried to stop once. And why bother trying to stop, eh? What's the point, guys? The point is this. Twenty-four of you are sitting here today, but the statistics are against you. Eight of you will die from this disease, eight of you will survive but decide to do some more research and eventually relapse at some point – and eight of you will 'get it'. You'll turn your lives around and head in a healthy direction, you'll thrive! Addiction is a disease of forgetfulness and complacency, but first and foremost, it's terminal.'

I looked around the room, at the housewife whose skin was just hanging on to her face by the cheekbones; at the yellow skin of the plastic surgeon who was one drink away from making his liver explode; then at the young African man with a scarf permanently wrapped round half of his face because he couldn't bear to unmask himself. I looked at Jimmy, who was looking at me, and I looked back at him with the same 'oh shit' expression as his, neither of us knowing which of the three categories we fell into. I stared down at my crooked toes, poking through my sandals, and wondered if my feet had the strength to carry me out of rehab alive. I knew one thing. I only had the strength to give this one shot: no way could I pick myself up from a relapse.

For five days I was confined to the grounds of the rehab. No phone calls or trips to the local shops. Even if I'd wanted to run away I didn't have the courage to explore the unfamiliar local area. Occasionally I'd wonder where Crow was. He paid me no more attention, but I could hear his excited caw every morning in the car park.

Mark was having a few more encounters of his own. Crow's excitement was always followed by hearing him walk into the staff office cursing to the others about crows shitting on him every time he got out of his car. On one occasion I passed him in the hallway as he was wiping bird crap from his glasses again.

'What the hell! If I get shat on one more time I'll…' he said, flummoxed by what course of action he could take to protect himself from the daily bombardment of shit. There was a tremor in his voice, hinting he was close to tears.

Word spread of Mark's plight. While some of the clients found it highly amusing, I couldn't see anything funny about my or anyone else's predicament. Mark had a job to do and he was doing it very well, actually; he'd found a way in. Instead of flying off Beachy Head I had decided to use the runway at Heathrow Airport. Flying the white flag, I surrendered – almost. All I had to do was walk into the group therapy room and sit on a chair; most times I started crying before the counsellors arrived. Each session would start in the same silent manner. They walked in, sat down and waited for someone to start talking, or in my case blubbing. Most times I'd get in first; I couldn't wait, eager to shed the embarrassment and guilt. Every time I finished sharing an account of how I'd hurt myself or someone else, I felt lighter, cleaner. I had another motive though, my family were doing their best to write the collateral letters counsellors asked them to send in.

The more I could remember now, the less ammo

they'd have to hit me with – not that they needed it. I could still feel the cat scratching inside. Tearing at my flesh: how the rawness hurt. No drugs to hide behind anymore.

I didn't recognise the person I talked about, the impostor who'd taken over my body and mind, wreaking havoc on everyone and everything I'd ever known, doing his best to destroy any chance of a future I might have. The druggy disguise didn't work anymore. I washed it away with the tears which flowed from my new eyes.

After five days spent in the perimeters of the rehab I was given permission to walk to the local Seven Eleven. A five-minute stroll consisting of a right turn out of the drive past the robots, an endearing South African name for British traffic-lights, before negotiating a level-crossing to a car park flanked by the Banana Jam Bar Grill. A diagonal line through the car park led to the Seven Eleven in a row of shops consisting of an internet cafe, a sports bar and a barber. Equipped with a hundred and fifty rand from everyone's allowance and a shopping list of cigarettes, chocolate and sodas, I made my way through the gliding electric gates with Cassie as my reluctant chaperone.

She hated being delegated for the lunchtime shopping trip, not because of laziness, but because she felt safe staying away from the temptations of the internet cafe. Every computer connected to the internet had the potential to trigger her cravings. We weren't such different people even though our drugs of choice took different forms. Just as my preference moved from marijuana, to alcohol, to cocaine, and finally back to alcohol as my tolerance killed each buzz until absolutely nothing worked, Cassie had her own encounters. Gorging and purging on food was replaced by an unhealthy interest in diet pills and fat-burners until she ended up in intensive care with major organ failure. Her discharge triggered a cross-addiction to endorphins released by her body when she cut into her skin. When that started to lose its novelty she found infatuation with social networking sites, trumped by Facebook. I'd heard of it from my dealer. He tried to get me to use it as a more covert way of arranging our rendezvous as the tools of his trade began to infect him with paranoia about an eternally imminent drug bust, but his plan was futile as I couldn't sit in front of a computer, let alone log on to the internet, petrified that the all-seeing eye of the worldwide web would incriminate me. I was curious to know how someone could get addicted to something other than a substance which required physical consumption.

We crossed the air-conditioned threshold of the rehab into the raw sunshine. Blurred frequencies of heat-haze quivered above the tarmac, scanning my body as I walked through the dense air. Usually just a distant rumble heard from behind the clinic walls, the stampeding sound of midday activity hit me. Pathetic squeaking taxi horns from ancient rusted Volkswagen Transporters, drowned out by the hollers of their drivers and fare collectors competing for the next passenger. Traffic and people everywhere: I'd underestimated the shock to my senses as they came back to life. I drew closer to Cassie for security as we waited at the curb for the green man. The back of my wrist brushed against her forearm, once, twice. She didn't move away. It felt like touching someone for the first time. The euphoric recall Elizabeth mentioned showed itself as a luscious absinthe-green light beckoning me from the side of the road.

'What's the deal with this Facebook thing then, Cassie?' I said.

She stopped in her tracks. 'Don't tell me you've never heard of Facebook?' She gripped my shoulder in disbelief.

'I've heard of it, just never used it.'

'Fuck me, you must be the only one,' she said, releasing her fingers, slowly letting them brush against my biceps.

'I've got a different phobia about computers. It may have gone now I've stopped the cocaine, but I'm not ready to check that one out.'

Cassie became distracted; she scratched at the long sleeve of her left arm, nervously humming a Bryan Adams tune, distracting herself from the approaching threat of the internet cafe. 'Now it cuts like a knife, but it feels so right. Hmm mmm… now it cuts like a knife, but it feels soooo right.'

'What's up with your arm?' I said.

Cassie held the cuff of the sleeve, debating whether to pull it up.

'Ah what the heck, this is what's up!' She pulled the sleeve high up her arm to reveal several scabs and scars of the word 'like', etched with what looked like implements of varying sharpness, from the deep precision lines of a razor-blade to the ragged lines of an eating knife.

'What the hell happened there?' A surge of nausea rose from my stomach, and the backs of my legs fell away from my body at a million miles an hour: a feeling I'd never been able to explain. It hit whenever I found something revolting and no one I'd ever met could empathise with me so I kept it to myself.

'Facebook got the better of me. You could say I hit the 'wall'. Check this one out. I did it in the mirror. What a dick, eh?'

I hoped she was asking a rhetorical question, as it was laughable. Cassie had cut the word 'like' into the only part of her arm she couldn't see properly without a mirror. It spelt 'ekil'.

'All I wanted was some approval,' she said, distracted from the cafe's blatant cyber threat no more than twenty yards away. Her face contorted as she went inside herself to search for more of an explanation. 'I just wanted people to like me, to know that I fitted in somewhere. The only friends I made at college were temporary ones. We got wasted together and went our separate ways. University was just the same, all I wanted to do was sing, but Mum and Dad just happened to pay for somewhere that didn't offer a music degree.' She scuffed her heel as she struck out at a stone. 'That's when I started to cut myself. I hated the place, it was huge. I didn't know how to make friends so I followed the Facebook crowd, but I found it so brutal. I couldn't handle the rejection if no one noticed my comments or photos. My adrenalin levels went through the roof, waiting to see whether anyone paid my page some attention, so I created a few fake accounts to increase my chances of Facebook popularity.'

Cassie, stunned that our conversation had helped her to bypass the internet cafe without realising it, looked at me, beaming the biggest smile I'd seen from anyone for months, maybe even years.

'Thank you, Aaron,' she said, suddenly stopping to put her arms around me. Her head pressed sideways against my chest, and I felt her breasts against my body.

'What for?' I said, half-heartedly putting one arm around her. Part of me wanted to grip her tightly, the other part wondered if I was betraying Karen more than I already had by my love affair with drugs and alcohol.

'For getting me past the cafe, and listening,' she said with a wink of an eye. As she released her hold, her right hand fell to the small of my back, smoothing the contour of my arse as she turned to walk on.

'You're very welcome,' I said, returning half a smile.

We were outside the sports bar. My stomach churned. People sat a few feet away from me drinking beer and cocktails. Premiere League football blared out of the widescreens inside. Irritation prickled over me as I watched a man raise his glass to his lips, fuelling his incessant laughter and flirtatious looks towards the woman opposite. It was the first time I'd seen alcohol since the end of our love affair. I looked at the bar through the open frontage of the building in all its polished wooden splendour. Once, my drinking eyes had greeted such a scene with excitement: an opportunity to leave reality through the thirsty portal in my mind. But I was an observer now, with no permission to participate anymore. I flashed back to a summer evening at The Shamrock pub. I'd walked past the bar on my way from the toilet, unable to enjoy a pleasant summer evening in the beer garden with friends, two friends whose own level of indulgence used to scare me, but time had twisted roles. I wanted more, more, more! More than them, more than anyone: 'just give me fucking more' was my mantra. By that time I constantly craved anything that removed me from reality and somehow I thought I possessed enough cunning to keep the extent of my deceit hidden from the rest of the world, and of course, me. If I couldn't get cocaine, a sly shot of tequila sufficed in satisfying the wanton need to distort my life. The magnetic pull of the bar sidetracked me. I went for the quick-draw shot, but my friend nabbed me.

'Karen would kill you if she found out,' he said, as I rested the glass as far away from me as possible. I didn't heed the warning. I didn't give a shit. I enjoyed the buzz of living on the edge and of taking self-sabotage to new levels. How far could I really go? The burn of the tequila felt so good.

I came back to the sports bar. No physical boundary stopped me from walking the twenty paces to the bar and ordering a neat triple gin, but something lurked in the half-light of the bar.

The Four Horsemen of my own apocalypse followed my progress. Urging me to fail at my attempt to re-join life, ready to take me squirming back to the straitjacket. Cigarette smoke caught streams of light as it billowed across the threshold of the darkened depths of the bar, where sordid thoughts lay stagnant in the alcohol-stained floorboards. I sensed evil's anticipation and entertained it ever so fleetingly. I sent my imagination to the bar's toilets, I felt the excitement as I locked myself in, that euphoria of reaching the solitude of the toilet cell, free to tip cocaine onto the toilet seat and hoof it up my nose for a burst of chemical-courage. But my nemesis arrived right on cue. My mind had triggered its self-defence mechanism to ward off my diseased daydreaming. All the arguments, slammed doors, tears and restless nights spent squirming away from Terror, Bewilderment, Frustration and Despair flooded back to me. Powerlessness was slowly imprinting its mark on me with the disclosures made in every group or one-to-one session. The more I shared, the more I remembered, and the list of damages seemed endless. Mark's words of warning from a morning lecture pulled me back to the light of day. 'Addiction is a progressive disease; if you pick up again, you'll be exactly where you left off.'

In that moment, outside the bar, I felt the truth in his words. I wasn't out of the woods yet, with such a short distance separating me from relapse, but self-preservation got the better of me. A new strength supported me, new light guided me away from the shadows and a friendly voice spoke to me.

'Aaron, are you okay?' Cassie said, 'You look like you've seen a ghost.'

'You're not far off there,' I said. My feet decided to move. The Horsemen retreated and waited; they were good at waiting. Bewilderment left me with the tormenting sight of a couple leaving the bar, and my eyes scanned back to their table to find half-full glasses abandoned with flippant disregard for the wasted alcohol. I was stunned at the idiocy of anyone who would walk away from anything but an empty glass; insanity was everywhere.

'I was just thinking about how fucked-up things got, I doubt I'll ever see Karen again.'

'No shit, things must've been screwed for you to end up out here,' Cassie said.

We exchanged smiles, mine half-faked. I couldn't allow myself the privilege of happiness, but there was a glimmer of hope in the upturned corners of my mouth; a sense of humour still existed and just might rise again.

I shivered in the heat at the thought of having to live with my parents again under constant suspicion. How could trust be rebuilt after so much damage?

We left the Seven Eleven with two bags of comfort-supplies consisting of sugar and cigarettes. I'd never been a chain smoker and my own thoughts about smoking confirmed what others said about me if they saw me with a cigarette. It didn't suit me. It never felt right, but I needed something to take the place of booze and cocaine more than ever. The first cigarette of the day after a hearty breakfast gave me the most satisfying dizzy head-rush as the arsenic and carbon-monoxide sucked the oxygen out of my bloodstream. I was never able to duplicate that elusive first hit of cocaine, and true to form I kept searching for that nicotine buzz all day long, convincing myself I was still getting something other than cancer.

'Have you ever felt like killing yourself, Aaron, you know, properly? None of this half-arsed shit with drugs?' Cassie said. As we headed back to rehab, an armoured vehicle the size of a tank pulled up at the shop to take the money to the bank. A uniformed guard with an Uzi machine gun waited alertly for his colleague to do the run.

'About four weeks ago I pulled the map out to look at the route to Beachy Head; it's a favourite cliff by the English Channel for jumpers. I knew the only way to numb the twisting of my guts every morning was to score some more coke, but I began hating myself so much I thought it would be a quick way to check out of life completely instead of hiding and slugging myself to death with shit drugs and cheap gin. A dealer's text message sidetracked me and I went for the score instead. Why do you ask?'

'I feel like killing myself every day. It's the first thing I think about when I open my eyes in the morning. I ask myself – 'have you got the guts today, Cassie?' Then I think about how I might like to leave this world. Quickly, under a train, or slowly in a fireball at a petrol station; that's the current favourite, it would get me used to the heat of hell.'

Cassie timed her words perfectly. We arrived at the level crossing as the gates descended. Crowds gathered on each side of the tracks; most prominent were the women laden with shopping. Their infants were secured on their backs and fronts by cloth slings as colourful as the trademark loud animated voices, indigenous to well-fed big-breasted African women. Their journeys were temporarily halted, no one minding a five-minute delay in the drifting African time.

Cassie tapped her knuckles on the metal in perfect time with the suicide-bomb ticking inside her head, but she could never push the button. She looked tormented by the door opened by the counsellors' efforts, which showed her a new way, without self-inflicted pain, but she wasn't ready to let go. We had all been told that the statistics were stacked against us, that it was never going to be easy, but the solution was simple. With hard work, recovery promised a new life with unspeakably beautiful gifts. I wondered if her scarred limbs had any strength left to make it. Or maybe the cop out of suicide seemed the most sensible option instead of trying, failing and disappointing her parents again. I looked at her shaking hands as her eyes flitted down both directions of the tracks. The bomb ticked louder… tick tick tick.

'Cassie, you okay?' But she was off with the fairies. Recovery's door closed, hell's opened. She appeared to hear only the distant rumble of the train, her ears honed in, all else excluded. Her legs started shaking. She gave a small anxious wince, but there seemed to be pleasure in the pain, as if she was addicted to the adrenalin of deathly drama.

'Hold these, take them back, 'case I don't make it.' She shoved the bags at my chest and gripped the barrier with both hands, looking back at me with tears in her eyes.

'What the fuck are you doing?' I said.

'I ask myself that all the time.' Cassie's face was full of torment and confusion; tears free-flowed down her freckled cheeks. For a split second she seemed to experience a change of heart; she relaxed her grip and took half a step back, but it was as if something twisted in her gut. 'See you on the other side, Aaron.'

I didn't know if she referred to the tracks or to death. Seemingly powerless to control the urge, she flung her legs sideways over the barrier. The train drew closer – fifty yards, forty yards, thirty, twenty – and Cassie darted like a greyhound from its trap across the tracks. I tried to shut my eyes, but the morbidity of the moment got the better of me. The driver blasted his horn, and carriages fled past to reveal Cassie staring at me from the other side of the barrier. She wiped the tears from her face with the cuff of her jumper, frantically breathing, on the edge of hyperventilation, and then she turned and shouted.

'Better than any drug you ever took, loser!'

I watched Cassie disappear through the waiting crowd, heads turning, muttering in disbelief. I knew the confused space Cassie was in; I'd tried many a time to stop drinking. Karen and I had visited the doctor and three different counsellors she'd found to try and help me. I'd clicked with one of the counsellors; his neuro-linguistic programming approach worked for a short time. I found two weeks of peace and calm during which I was able to reconnect in some small way with my soul, but I wasn't ready, things weren't bad enough, and I needed to do more research into how bad I could get them; I had to find rock bottom. I was desperate to know how low I could sink. Cassie was still testing the limits. I followed her red hair until she turned into the rehab; I couldn't take my eyes off her. The crazy glint in her eye lingered over me, making me want her even more.

The last carriage of the train clattered away, barriers lifted, conversations paused as the women picked up their shopping. I started walking the twenty-foot gap between the rails, instinctively looking down each length of track to make sure I was out of the danger I saw Cassie flirt with. As I straightened my head I was greeted with a shriek and a tumbling of plastic bags bowling their fruit and vegetables. Apples hit my feet, potatoes nutmegged my legs as the lady carrying them tripped on the rails, her outstretched hands landing at my feet as her knees and elbows thudded against the unyielding concrete. The next minutes engraved themselves on my mind.

I knelt down to offer her my hand. She looked up with her round black face, unable to move from the shock at finding herself on the ground. Children scampered for the rolling apples in front of the hooting traffic. The lady's surprise at seeing a white hand helping her was blatant, but instead of a look of fright or dismissal, her aghast jaw closed and she beamed a smile with rays of gratitude right at me.

'Thank you,' she said, taking my hand, pulling herself to her feet. That was the extent of our exchange: nothing more than a helping hand received, nothing less than the first 'thank you' I'd received for months, having done nothing of merit for anyone other than myself. The woman's gratitude lightened the soles of my feet as I made my way back to rehab, brushing the palms of my hands against fresh leaves. I found a memory as I walked on.

I couldn't place the time in my life, but I knew it existed; vivid images played in my mind, fuelled by the good deed life had synchronised for me. I flashed back to a huge white horse standing in the garden of a dilapidated house, once home to the King of Romania's daughter. The house had three floors, each with wrap-around balustrade balconies. Its ornate roof, once gold-plated peaks crowning the building in opulence, had warped and faded into disrepair. The whole experience would've been a fairy tale, but for the conditions the disabled children lived in. I was visiting an orphanage to expand my horizons and get a burst of life-experience. I wasn't prepared for the deprived conditions eighty-two severely disabled children were living in, though. Banished by Nicolae Ceauşescu's brutal regime to live in villages far away from everyone else, they were labelled 'devil's children'. I recalled my night-time walk around Bucharest before I arrived at the orphanage with the school teachers and priest I was travelling with;

heavy artillery bullet holes peppered the communications building. We walked into a derelict building site where a ten-year-old boy asked us for money to buy more glue to sniff, and as we left, an even younger boy was sitting at the base of a traffic light pole, begging. Abandoned children were everywhere. The orphanage haunted me. The mile-long road leading to the orphanage in the small peasant town of Czienne was lined with telegraph-poles, half their lengths painted white to celebrate Easter. Each pole held a huge stalk nest; some had long beaks gaping over the edge, waiting expectantly for food. All the towns in rural locations received plumbed hot water on different days of the week, with electricity rarely being available for all twenty-four hours of the day.

The children slept in severely overcrowded quarters, three to a single bed. Their food was slopped out in a basement, overseen by the oldest and most able boy, Pinocchio. He had a large stick to keep order with when the children broke free from the inexperienced nursing team. None of the staff interfered with his authority, as he made their life easier, but it was the white horse which came most vividly back to me.

Pinocchio was the only person the horse would let near him or on his back. I sat in the long grass playing with the children, watching them ride around the grounds. Whenever I was outside the horse would find me and stare at me. If I decided to approach, he stamped his front feet, dipping and shaking his head in annoyance. While I couldn't remember when in my life I'd visited the orphanage, I knew it was in my long hippy-hair days as the children unpredictably launched themselves onto my back, Tarzan-style, pulling clumps of hair clean out of my head. Pinocchio became intrigued by his pet's interest in me. My lack of skill in the Romanian language left me gesticulating to him every time he tried to move the horse away from me. His hooves stood fast and his muscular neck shook off Pinocchio's attempts to pull him away. There was a familiarity between us, an unspoken connection, but he saw something in me which made him uneasy, jittery; maybe he sensed the junkie on my back. He wanted to introduce himself, but sensed I hadn't banished my demons. I was yet to descend into the darkness of addiction. An animal so white and pure wasn't going to be tainted by illness.

On my last day at the orphanage I sat with the children for the last time; chilled evening air giving birth to droplets of dew coating waist-high meadow grass. The horse watched me say goodbye to the staff. He disappeared from view for the first time I could remember since my arrival. The priest arrived to take me back to Bucharest, but the horse wanted to say his own farewell. I listened to his slow, heavy steps brush through the grass behind me. Pinocchio was nowhere in sight. The horse's breath reached the back of my neck, misting as it flowed around me, catching beams of the orange setting sun which filtered through the trees surrounding the garden. He stood still behind me, and goosebumps made the hairs on the back of my neck stand to attention. The priest's horn hooted, prompting an annoyed grunt from my four-legged inquisitor as he pressed his warm soft nose against my back, gently nudging me forward. I plucked up the courage to stand and face him. We stood face to face for what I thought would be the last time. I held the look in his beautiful black eyes, and my hand instinctively touched his soft cheek. He pressed it to the palm of my hand, closing his eyes as if remembering, and as I closed my eyes a shiver of energy pulsed down my spine filling me with bursts of fear and sadness. I saw myself surrounded by darkness, lost in the shadows. I moved to pull my hand away but the energy held me still. Warmth flooded my body with a strength of love I'd never felt before. Tears streamed down my cheeks; I screwed my eyes tightly shut trying to block their flow, the desperate vision disappeared, and I was left knowing that the time of shadows was years ahead of me. He wanted me to know the love I'd given the orphans was there for me, too; I felt his thoughts. He wanted me to know that I wasn't alone, that I'd never be alone because he has always been there and would be with me for eternity in ways my life had not yet come to experience. I wasn't ready for the magic. I wasn't ready to experience the beauty of the light because I hadn't found the darkness, but it was coming.

The priest sounded the horn again, keen to find his way through the potholed roads before night fell. I stroked my palm down the horse's white cheek.

'Goodbye,' I said softly. I never returned to Romania, but it wasn't goodbye.

The horse couldn't let me leave without showing me why he was so wary of me when I arrived. He met with me on his terms to show me a glimpse of the challenges ahead. The junkie hadn't found me in Romania; the vision saw me healthy. I soon chose the lonely fork in the road leading to the edge, but while those days were dark and desperate, now I found myself walking in the South African sunshine, surfacing for clean air. Piece by piece my history was being revealed to me. As I turned into the rehab gates, I was stopped in my tracks as my ears were suddenly filled with the deep pounding rhythm again, but louder than before. I held my head in my hands shielding me from the 'BOOM BOOM BOOM!' and then it stopped. The security guard stared at me as I hurried back to my room before it hit me again.

SIX

'It's just like peeling an onion,' Jimmy said as we sat on the sun-baked paving by the small tear-drop shaped swimming pool, our oasis in the middle of treatment, reached by a pathway which led from the gardens between a perimeter wall and the side of the rehab. Double helpings of lunch made chain smoking more satisfying. The rush-hour boom of traffic and trains were a constant reminder that real life still existed outside the rehab walls.

'They strip you bare to the core, taking off all that stinking flesh, stirring the sludge up so you can find out what's in the middle, who you really are!' Jimmy said. His leg jigged nervously up and down five times a second, and then he leapt to his feet for a nervous circuit of the garden chuffing like a steam-train. I couldn't help but compare his behaviour to someone on amphetamines, but discounted the thought as a result of my paranoia and a genuine fondness for the guy. For all his jumpiness, Jimmy was trying hard to get to know me, and I hadn't had normal social conversations with people for longer than I could remember. There was a sincerity behind his damage. He had total lulls in his behaviour where it seemed as if a switch flicked and he took on the appearance of a calm, composed gentleman. He had a lull that day by the pool. He returned to sit down with me after his steam-train circuit of the pool.

'What happened, Aaron, how did it get so bad?' he said.

'Not sure, I just slipped down this slope that got steeper as time went on. I spent most of my teenage years and early twenties on a tennis court; I loved the game. Five, six days a week I played; just having the occasional beer after a game. When I tried marihuana things changed. I had to have the stuff with me, like an essential accessory. I couldn't imagine being without it; I felt inadequate without it. When I went to America and Canada to coach tennis for a couple of years I drank so much my bowels got inflamed, and I started passing blood when I got home. I calmed down for a while, until I met Karen. We had a lot of fun going to parties every weekend and a few festivals every summer, it was a complete blast. I can remember feeling like I was losing my grip a bit, like I wanted to say no to people but didn't know how. Karen had a huge group of friends, really colourful funny characters, you know, larger than life. When I drank or did drugs I felt like I was fitting in more, like I could step out of myself and let go, but I just drifted further away from who I really was.

Jimmy's arm didn't feel disgusting when he put it round my shoulders. 'It's okay, buddy, c'mon, it's time for the share.' He patted me on the back as we moved to the lounge. I had the utmost respect for him at that moment, knowing that all I needed was some company, not conversation. We walked into the square high-ceilinged lounge and sat with twenty-four recovering addicts, squashed into sofas, listening to a former patient who began to tell us his story of experience, strength and hope. Mine was just beginning, and the more people I listened to, I realised that I wasn't so special or different from anyone else who found themselves in rehab. Self-seeking began to slip away.

After the share I returned to the unlit bedroom. My hand froze at the light switch, just as it did every evening as my head entertained the possibility that if Crow had followed me from England, maybe the IRA terrorist was still at large. I sat on my bed with a writing pad and the Big Book, mulling over whether to start my life story or read a book which talked about finding God and asking Him to grant me serenity. Neither option felt very attractive. My perception of God was still tainted by attendance at Catholic Church with my dad, who eventually let me make up my own mind whether to spend an hour of my weekend staring at a giant painting of Jesus surrounded by the wrath of thundering skies as rain washed blood from his stigmata and thorn-punctured head. I never understood why children were allowed to see such gruesome scenes and were taught about guilt and not being 'worthy enough to eat the crumbs from under thy table' – but as I looked back, I remembered the stillness that rose from a hundred people to the giant beams of the chapel as the priest invited everyone into prayer. My promotion from a member of the congregation to altar boy graced me with access to the church wine, giving me an enthusiastic spring in my step as I walked to my dad's car for the weekly service. I took to the taste like a duck to water. The sweet blood of Christ was certainly very palatable, making the hymns a tad livelier and the time flow faster. Half-heartedly, I opened the book and made an effort to read something, but my eyes danced uncontrollably over the words, racing to the end of the page without taking in any information.

I was still clean and the tears kept falling, but it seemed that success in rehab also depended on being studious and learning new subjects. Academically I had failed miserably at school, despite my dad's best efforts to help me with his own style of incredibly patient tuition. I didn't even know what the word sobriety meant until I got to Cedar Ridge. I'll never forget the look on Jimmy's face when I asked him what it meant. He just stared at me in shock, with a look which spelt out his thoughts very clearly.

'You don't stand a hope in hell,' was telegraphed right to me.

Jimmy bounced into the room and got undressed like his clothes were on fire. Addiction had turned us both into night owls. Before psychosis had begun to drive me insane, I welcomed the night. While everyone else slept I was more assured of being undisturbed as I took cocaine and invited strange presences into my room to join in my mayhem, while my skin crawled with chemical pleasure. Jimmy was no different; we had so much in common with our using, which was so prolific that neither of us stood a chance in hell of finding a natural rhythm of day and night. To be able to quell his restless disposition, Jimmy wrapped himself tightly into his bed with the sheets tucked under the mattress and a special thick weighted blanket, the type used to comfort autistic children, placed over him. Every few minutes the relentless sound of his tossing and turning disturbed my rest. Next door, snoring vibrated the wall. Ben, a sixty-something Scottish guy, had been banished to a room of his own. No one could sleep in the same room as the elephant. I had some sympathy for him once I found out his lungs were diseased from asbestos poisoning. He had relapsed after thirty years of sobriety. Unable to let go of the resentment against his employers for 'putting him out to pasture', forcing his retirement, he hit the bottle big time. His liver was one more drink away from calling last orders.

As I lay in my bed with the elephant on one side and Jimmy deciding to desperately rub away for that all-elusive orgasm in an effort to find sleep in the afterglow, I habitually ran my hand down the side of the bed. My mannerisms still retained the memory of searching for wraps of cocaine I'd stashed under the mattress so I could slope off to the toilet and snort through the night, fuelling fantasies before the buzz crashed and the spectres started to move in from the shadows, turning my ecstasy to terror. In the weeks leading up to the trip to Lourdes my track record for inappropriate behaviour was growing longer by the day. I couldn't admit or deny anything anymore; diluted bottles of wine were poured to guests as most of the alcohol soaked into my stomach lining. My eyes focused on other women with unfaithful intent. I had lost all sense of certainty, unable to deny or admit to any of my misdemeanours with conviction.

I knelt on my bed and pushed myself between the curtains and window, resting my elbows on the ledge to take in the night air, just as I had done during my most desperate hours back home before stubbing the cigarette on my hand. Stars began to pierce holes through the black cloth sky. The moon's glow was turned on and off by the broken curtain of clouds and by Crow's black wings as they suddenly enveloped my full range of vision. I clung onto the ledge to stop myself falling backwards off the bed.

'Jeez! You could've warned me! What the hell are you doing flying at night, anyway? You're not an owl,' I said.

'I came from the same place as you, Aaron. From the darkness,' he replied, tapping his beak on the window next to my eyes with the slightest of pecks. The glass splintered, making a vertical zigzag five inches long, and then he was gone. As I stared at the crack the heaviness filled my head again: 'boom, boom, boom!' I flopped on my bed, pillow at the ready to muffle my hearing and block out the sound I'd heard during my childhood nightmares as the ogre's giant footsteps came looking for me. But while the sound was the same, this time I was awake, and instead of it signalling impending doom, I felt it calling out to me to come and find it.

I raised the pillow off with both hands and slipped it gently under my head. The window stayed open, letting the Cape Doctor in to softly brush my face; my eyes closed, ready for sleep. 'Boom, boom, boom': it came one last time – not from my head, but from far beyond the homes and trees lining the foothills of Table Mountain.

It was impossible to have any qualms about the grounds for Karen wanting a divorce: my 'unreasonable behaviour', as the court described it, was the perfect understatement. My pen hesitated over the dotted line of a document her lawyer had sent to Cape Town, so I could sign away my half of the house; I wasn't in any doubt about signing, but I couldn't remember what my signature looked like. My fist cracked the plastic biro in frustration at being relentlessly stripped of my identity. I made a child's scribble vaguely resembling my name and sealed the envelope.

While my body was beginning to heal and my heart to feel, my head was still a hectic, noisy place. It chit-chattered away about complete and utter bollocks; the speed and bizarreness of my thoughts were catastrophically creative. My imagination became more vivid than ever, creating its own unique dimension where my debauched thoughts ran rampant, creating scenes perfect for full-length disaster movies. The sickness of self-sabotage still pulled me towards negativity and destructiveness even if I had other ideas of a new life.

As the thirty-day programme neared conclusion the counsellors increased the pressure. I sat opposite the head doctor, Henrick, and prepared myself for a grilling. He was an interesting man to look at and listen to. His Indian origins suited Cape Town's multi-coloured population, and his Hindi accent was spiked with occasional South African twangs. His Porsche stood proud in a personal parking space, a just reward for cornering the rehab market in Cape Town. Porches weren't really my style, but Henrick's success still reassured me that it was possible to climb high after stooping so low, and he had definitely found his rock bottom. His hands and sandal-clad feet puffed out like rubber gloves filled with water. At the end of his active addiction, all the veins that had once been available to him to inject into had collapsed from repetitive needle-stabbing. The only places left to get the heroin in were under his fingernails and toenails, hence the bloated extremities of his body. He had to inject himself with medication every few days to keep the pain at bay. He called it his 'lifelong penance', and he usually knew the score when it came to spotting if someone was ready to change – but he seemed puzzled by me.

'You're a bit of conundrum, Aaron, you know that, don't you?' he said, gently chewing the end of his pen.

'You'll probably have to expand a little.' I gave a nervous smile, still unable to grant myself the happiness of a genuine one.

'The team think you're flying under the radar. They reckon you have a force-field around you, hiding something,' he replied, laughing at the ridiculousness of the idea. His eyes danced around me, searching for it. 'They've seen your tears – no one doubts they're genuine – but we don't know much else about you. Your life story is a week overdue. Procrastination's just another symptom of this disease, eh? The more open you are, the more we can help you, man. Everyone has a story to tell; it may have been ugly for you, but we still need to hear it.'

'I'm not hiding anything. I know how I got here, I know why I'm here and why my wife is divorcing me, but all my memories are broken pieces. I'm so confused. I remember fragments of my childhood – having an accident as a one-year-old which only came to me the other day, for the first time ever. It scared the shit out of me! Memories of my adolescent years consist of an overwhelming sense of psychic perception, sounds, sights, people's feelings and thoughts used to just rock-slide down on me. I couldn't tell you guys that stuff or you'd cart me off to the psych unit. And you know what the scary thing is?'

'No, tell me,' Henrick said.

'I can feel all that coming back to me now and I don't know what I should be doing with it.'

Henrick recognised my confusion. 'Hey man, don't fret. While procrastination is a very common symptom for an addict, so is memory loss. Alcohol attacks the hippocampus of your brain which is responsible for your short and long-term memory, so recalling memories and connecting them together, as well as retaining new ones, can be a challenge to say the least. That's just one theory. Another is that alcohol causes Korsakoff's amnesic syndrome, a brain disorder that produces symptoms of amnesia, attention deficit, and disorientation.'

'Shit,' I said, as I realised the extent of the damage I might have caused to my brain. I pondered on my inability to read even one page of a book from top to bottom, and the way I had to delve deep on how to tie a shoe lace.

'Listen, Aaron, many alcoholics are psychic or clairvoyant or something of that ilk. Many alcoholics don't recognise the gift they're given. They kill it with drugs, but others hear the calling so strong they can't deny it. Your journey has just begun, man; your life is about to start for the second time. I know you're certain of this direction, your tears aren't crocodile's. Look inside, you have to. This time, right here in Cape Town, it's your chance for a second incarnation: a personal reinvention. Not many people get to see that, let alone live all they dream to be. When I was two weeks clean I couldn't walk or hold anything without freaking from the pain of needle damage. My memories left me, and with them, pieces of my soul. I know that's happened to you. Some came back to me as I healed, some still prefer to stay hidden in safety, uncertain they will be able to trust me ever again. We are spiritual beings in a material world and this is a spiritual programme, Aaron. It's all about rejuvenation of the spirit.

To heal we need to change from way outside ourselves. Change the people you meet and hang out with. Most of them will go of their own accord, huh? Consequences, my friend. Change the places you go to and even where you live. Some of you Brits never go home; some have little to go back for. You need to change the things you do, but…' he leaned forward, holding his swollen finger up to make sure I got the message, '…the biggest change has to come from within. Find your spirit, your own power. Kill the sickness and feed off its flesh. It can nourish you, man. Turn the tables on this fucker and make it work for you. Use it as a launch pad to planet destiny!' Henrick stopped, suddenly aware of his theatrics.

'You've lost me a bit. What launch pad?' I said.

'Ha, sorry, man. Y'know why there are so many rehabs in Cape Town?'

'I didn't know there were. All I've seen is this place and the Seven Eleven.'

'It's that's rock, man – Table Mountain.'

'I haven't had a good look at it yet.'

'All the more reason to stick around. Take my advice and get over to Calloway House. Spend as much time as you need; you'll know when it's time to move on. Just don't hide here. Some stay because it's safe – heck! We look after you guys, don't we? Most people give secondary at least two months. What's another two months out of the rest of your life? Get to know the mountain. More importantly, let it get to know you.'

I began to wonder if Henrick had ever recovered. His

lectures to the clients were enlightening; his medical knowledge of the way addicts can get stuck in a vicious circle of dopamine withdrawals, endlessly searching for that elusive first-hit-buzz, gave me a rational, biological explanation for my monstrous greed. He also explained that alcohol was my drug of choice, my numero uno, and that cocaine just gave me the stamina to join up the dots and drink more. It made perfect sense when he put it like that.

While he may have been a little eccentric, Henrick's words stirred something. I remembered my brief glimpse of Table Mountain from the plane before landing. Still tranquillized by sadness and whisky, I felt nothing from the beauty of the site below me, but as the captain's pre-landing announcement prompted me to open my eyes, I caught the perfect snapshot of the rock jutting out of the Western Cape. The city poured out of the slopes of the mountain, birthed by the mother of all rocks. Cape Town: the Mother City.

'What's the plan, Stan?' Henrick's voice called me back to the second most important decision of my life. Would I surrender to the counsellors with faith that their personal experience of a disease I was only just coming to terms with could pull me up to new heights? Or maybe I'd had enough treatment in the bank to go back to England, and Cedar Ridge was just a machine with no heart, making money from Brits who, thanks to a generous exchange rate, could afford five grand worth of rehab treatment for a fifth of the British pound? I was learning to trust my gut;

after years of compulsive behaviour I began to know what felt right. I had nothing to lose by staying, and everything to gain. Besides, I felt safe where I was, as part of a group, with most of us on a mission to heal. The South African summer was about to kick off – beaches and bikinis in a city where the ratio of women to men was seven to one. The decision was becoming very easy to make as the sun rose on a new season and a new life.

'I'm staying. Just tell me what I need to do.' I put my trust in Henrick and his team of counsellors, and in doing so I started to take some real responsibility for myself again.

'Lekker, man,' he said.

'Lekker,' I replied as I smiled my first genuine smile for years and it shone back at him.

SEVEN

On the twenty-fifth day of rehab, five days before my move to Calloway House, I waited in the car park with Jimmy and Cassie for a ride to a meeting. The people-carrier surprised me by coming from the opposite direction for a change.

'Shotgun!' Jimmy shouted, sprinting for the front seat, clutching his green and gold Narcotics Anonymous recovery textbook. He never left for a meeting without the corresponding literature; if it wasn't green and gold, his nose would be buried in the Big Book.

'C'mon, buddy, you're always riding shotgun. Give us a ride up there,' I said.

'Acceptance is the answer to all your problems, Aaron. Comply or die, ha ha!' He reeled off another quote from his extensive repertoire. I couldn't help admiring how he had managed to focus his obsessive, compulsive behaviour on something healthy. I could tell the words he read were propelling him in the right direction, away from hell. And while I felt safer in rehab, I couldn't connect with the written work or literature, and frequently found myself lingering on the memory of just how good my last beer had tasted.

Cassie joined me on a back seat big enough for four people. My arm dangled from the open window as we left the electric gates. I felt her looking at me and turned my head to exchange smiles. She shuffled along the seat, checking to see if Jimmy or the driver noticed, before planting her arse and bare legs right next to mine. Her small cut-off jean-shorts dripped frayed white cotton strands over her skin. The warmth of her leg against mine tantalized me. My hand suddenly developed a mind of its own as I reached across to playfully flick the cotton, as if its position was annoying me. Cassie was quick to press her hand on mine, preventing me from removing it from her leg. I didn't resist. My fingers played guitar with the long thin ridge of a cutting scar I found on the lower reaches of her thigh, occasionally ever so slightly prying open the gap between the jeans and her skin, edging towards her centre.

Our destination was Constantia Narcotics Anonymous meeting. The narcotics accent on the meeting made no difference to me. I considered alcohol to be as much a drug as any other, just legal, very popular and poisonous. We were sent to a combination of Alcoholics and Narcotics Anonymous Meetings; this was my fifth since arriving. The importance of sharing something at every meeting we went to was impressed on us by the counsellors. Those of us who shared received affirmations at community meeting the next day. My track record wasn't looking good with five meetings and no shares to my name.

I didn't need anyone to pile on the pressure and no one did because I was good at doing that myself. Addiction was just one way I made life difficult for myself.

As Henrick and the team clinically yet carefully peeled the layers of my onion with expert precision, I began to see that addiction to mind-altering substances was just one of the symptoms of an illness with which I was becoming more familiar, the more I healed. In a nutshell, I was just trying to change the way I felt. I had no recollection of what it felt to be myself for what seemed like a decade.

However difficult I found opening my mouth at meetings I still looked forward to them because I realised I wasn't alone. My selfish supposition that I had to be the only person in the world suffering so badly was stripped away, and as we finished each meeting holding hands in a circle to say the serenity prayer, the group's energy flowed through my hands. That feeling of unity and strength in numbers had started to give me my power back. I knew these were the people I needed to associate myself with for the time being to stay safe. I was heading for a new life which sobriety promised to those who actually got it. All I had to do was cross the fabled bridge to normal living. I wanted it bad.

The pressure was on to say something that night. I'd had the slogan 'nothing changes if nothing changes' drilled into my skull by all and sundry.

'Think about it like one of the process groups, mate,' Jimmy said. 'You said yourself how much lighter you felt after getting all that stuff about Karen off your chest, didn't you?'

'Yeah, I know, but it always feels like I'm about to do a parachute jump when I'm waiting for the last person to share. I always leave it one second too long.'

'Don't come back tonight kicking yourself, Aaron.'

'Turn on the radio, driver,' Cassie interrupted. 'This is our only chance to listen to music all week!'

Bob Marley's voice came on the radio. Cassie joined in with the opening lines, 'Could you be loved, and be loved'. Her harmony with Bob's sunny tones gave me goosebumps. The windows were down, and warm night air filtered into the car as we sang along with Cassie and Bob, sharing the first minutes of a good time I allowed myself to have, clean, without needing or wanting a drink. Just then I forgot about everything bad that had happened, lifted by reggae and companionship. This is promising, I thought to myself, as I plucked away on the scar in between Cassie's legs.

Constantia ranked as one of the richest suburbs in Cape Town, home to politicians and millionaires. Only the tips of the roofs were visible from the roads as most of the buildings were hidden behind huge old trees, up long drives, and behind iron gates with razor wire and security cameras.

The meeting was held in a basketball gymnasium on

Constantia College campus. Bob was ringing in my ears as I left the floodlit car park for the pathway to the gym, bathed in the spotlight of the new moon. I let the others walk ahead, as their chit-chat distracted me. I was getting to know who I was again after misspent time with the impostor who'd trashed my life. I was a stranger to myself, forging a new relationship with someone born from the fertile ashes of my self-destructive fire. I was beginning to like my own company.

The path was flanked by the wall of the gym on one side, and a football field on the other. The still night brimmed with the soundtrack of crickets. I stopped as I saw something in the field. An Indian tepee stood tall and proud in total solitude, the flap door closed. No cars parked for a college camp out, no exhibition sign, just a tepee. I flashed back to the time I'd been levelled by a cold. I lay on my bed and placed my hands on my stomach, drifting away for hours, as the heat from the energy flowing through my hands flooded my body. I floated in and out of various states of consciousness, feeling so tranquil, when a vision with colour and sharpness I've never witnessed before flashed into my head.

An Indian boy in a loincloth ran through waist-high grass, laughing in the sunshine. His black shoulder-length hair framed a smiling, brown-skinned face. The vision only lasted a few seconds, but I could see it, even now, after the chemicals had attempted to wipe my mind clean.

I never knew much about reincarnation, but my

reintroduction to the world after returning from the alcoholic wilderness opened my mind to the possibilities of a second incarnation in the same lifetime. I knew that boy was me. The idea satisfied a fascination with Native American Indians I'd felt forever.

There was already a connection, an innate knowing that I was related to the Indian culture in a way I was yet to understand. I told myself the tepee was probably some project run by the college. I wasn't taking leave of my sanity again. It looked so welcoming, and it felt like home but also dreamlike, far enough away in the space where the night began for its shape to become vague. As I turned to join the meeting, Crow's silhouette caught the corner of my eye; he had arrived to rest on a wooden strut poking from the chimney hole of the tepee, making sure he knew where I was, and I he.

We sat in a circle of seats about thirty metres in diameter. I started shitting myself as soon as I sat down, waiting for an opportune moment to chip in with something worthwhile. I waited, ever so slightly praying, for inspiration to arrive. Was I practising patience or procrastination? Real courage comes from stepping off the edge and having faith that whatever happens, something good can come of it. But silence between the shares was few and far between. Everyone had something to say. The clock's big hand glided its way to the end of sharing time. The night air warmed as summer commenced, coaxing my legs into shorts and feet into sandaled fresh air. I nervously rocked the flexible back of my plastic chair as the pressure mounted. Parachute jump time. Fear crept into my head: who would want to listen to anything I had to say, even if I had words to utter? 'Have the courage to change the things I can, dammit!' my head shouted at me. I tuned out, and focused on a guy sharing directly opposite me. He wore an eye-patch, and an inch of crisscrossed stitches wiggled their way out of his eye socket. Crutches rested on his plaster-cast leg.

'I woke up behind the wheel of a stolen car parked through a shop window. I pulled a shard of glass out of my eye and blood dripped onto the can of beer in my lap. I took a sip and thought, this isn't very good, and then I passed out,' he said.

No shit, Sherlock. His injuries made me look at my feet. I counted the broken toes, finishing on the left big toe fractured above and below the joint from shutting my foot in a stable door during a binge of cocaine, MDMA, gin and black absinthe. I could remember the exact details of what I took that night, but still lost crucial memories of my travels around the world.

Alcohol and drugs just signposted the way to injury; usually the crazier the concoction, the worse the injury. I'd dislocated my shoulder putting a shirt on from an ouzo-induced hangover. I couldn't lift my arm for two weeks. The bones in my left toe healed crooked after perilous drives to score more coke while I convalesced at home. I got into a vicious circle; it was the prime of my active addiction. The injuries gave me more time alone at home to get higher and, with each come-down, I sank lower towards rock-bottom.

Then there was a pause which opened up the sharing. It had my name on it. I waited for two more seconds, certain someone would take the silence, but no one did. I jumped from the plane, trusting the parachute would open with divine intervention. It did.

'I'm Aaron, I'm an alcoholic.' Formalities out of the way. 'Today I've been clean for twenty-five days. That's twenty-five days without cutting my skin or breaking any bones, no embarrassment, just hoping and knowing I am in the right place. I'm intact, this is the best I've felt for a very long time. Thanks for welcoming me and giving me something to hang on to, something to belong to. My marriage is broken, but we both got out alive, just. I'm healing… one day at a time. Thank you.'

'Thanks, Aaron,' everyone in the circle echoed back. Job done, I felt a surge of energy prickle into my hands and shoot up my spine. The top of my head buzzed. I closed my eyes to find the golden light sparkling on the darkened screen of my eyelids. A sense of peace, new to me, arrived, held by something: a power I trusted emphatically. I knew nothing, but that I was part of a spiritual programme recovering from a spiritual malady. The buzzing spread from the top of my head to my feet. It filled the room. The wind blew in from its spacious home in the darkness of night, through the open doors to the electric light of the room, momentarily filling the air with its sweeping sound, dancing with the golden sparkle. No one acted as though they saw the luminous spectacle – a personal gift from the great beyond, perhaps – or maybe everyone saw it as clearly as me. I didn't suppose that my sensitivities to energy and the elements were unique to me, but I hadn't yet found the confidence to initiate conversations with people and find out. My comfort zone was in quietness.

I caught the last share of the night. Contributions collected, and a final standing ovation to the serenity prayer. I understood the words in my own way, pleading for serenity from the confusion my head tried to feed me. I accepted I could never change the fact that drink and drugs had lost their joy; sure, I could try them again if I willed, but I had absolutely no idea what would happen afterwards, be it the gutter or not. The game was up: no fun down that avenue anymore. Courage seeped from my pores as I faced my apocalyptic demons, battling them and winning round twenty-five. So far so good. But wisdom was in short reserve, and right then the only wise thing to do was to stick with these guys. Everyone talked about trusting a process and following a way with nothing to fear. I stood shoulder to shoulder with people who had years of sobriety and clean living under their belts and bra straps. They looked strong and happy, smiling and laughing as if they really felt it. If it worked for them, it could work for me.

But whom was I saying the prayer to? From the shadows a light shone on memories of the richness of life. In Crow I had a guardian, once clouded by my crooked beer goggles. My God wanted me to know something.

The beauty of the twelve-step programme was in the artistic licence given to name God as who or whatever I pleased. A mountain goat or Buddha himself. I just had to believe, trust, and pray to this power for help to find happiness again. So I turned to Mother Nature and asked her to hold me and feed me from the lush soils of her womb. I began to walk on her skin with gratitude and love for a new life, so nearly wasted. I turned to the elements for inspiration. I found God in the Great Outdoors.

EIGHT

On my last night at Cedar Ridge I rested in my bed waiting for sleep to come, half-written pages of a life story scattered around me, crumpled from the frustration of not knowing how or what to write. Jimmy and Cassie had already left for Calloway House. The only person I had come to Cape Town to get to know was myself, but I had got to know them by default of being British and adopting the 'let's stick together' motto at a time in our lives when it was make or break. No one had filled Jimmy's bed yet. I found myself alone in the room; the nurses' station light spread around the corner of the landing, giving me a sense of security as it peeked through the bedroom door, left ajar at night. According to Elizabeth I'd been writhing and screaming in my sleep most nights since my arrival.

The shadows waited; they found me in my sleep when I was most vulnerable. Dreams of scoring cocaine and getting drunk fooled me into thinking I'd relapsed. I'd wake, sweating in horror, unable to tell whether I'd relapsed, until I grasped the reality of the waking day.

Propped up by pillows I sat with the Big Book resting on my lap; this was to be my last sleep before moving to secondary. The moon's light found me through the open curtains, and wind brushed through the branches filling the night air with its calming song. My copy of the Big Book remained untouched, but for my brief scans of people's alcoholic war stories and recoveries in the last half of the book, preceded by the story of the author, Bill Wilson, and his account of how the Twelve Steps came to be.

I flicked the pages of the book, curious to know where it would open. I joined the gifted page halfway down. My eyes jerked up, down, left and right, finally settling on Bill's most desperate moment, when the only thing he could do was pray from his secure hospital room for relief from the pain of insanity. He called out desperately, asking God for help from his knees, and a wind burst into his room, overcoming him with love and bringing with it a divine white light. Bill said he was saved that night and was relieved of his affliction. He found his way back again and with him came a gift to give to millions looking for relief from alcoholism.

I rested the book on my lap and stared into the darkest corner of the bedroom, but it wasn't black. The darker the room became, the more the golden light sparkled. I closed my eyes and listened to the wind, hearing it more clearly than ever. Throughout addiction I'd lost touch with the simplest forms of nature's beauty. Shying away from the sunlight, blotting out the moon and hiding from the wind – it searched for me to take me to blue sky heights and beyond to the stars so my spirit could be free. My inner light shone brightly behind my eyes, a brightness so intense it should have burnt my eyes but didn't, because it came from within me to make sure I never feared the dark again. Its presence kept me company: the darker the night, the brighter the light.

I walked to the toilet next to my bedroom, forgetting to pause at the light switch. My meditation with the wind and light had quietened my thoughts. I felt my strength increase every day and felt a reassuring presence near me. Whether I saw the golden light or not, I knew I was protected by something powerful and loving. I reached out to it, communing in silence, placing my will and my life in its care. As I washed my hands I met myself face to face in the mirror. My ill reflection had faded. The sunshine coaxed out freckles. There was something different about the person facing me in the mirror. The first signs of a personal transformation I could only see once I'd risen from the fertile ashes of my destructive fire.

Calloway House was a bit of a conundrum for me. On the one hand the six-bedroom detached house was completely different from Cedar Ridge's clinical, office-like environment. It was at the end of a dirt track a few minutes' walk from the Seven Eleven which lay equidistant between the two rehabs. A wood-slatted security hut marked the entrance to the dirt lane; it was manned every evening until morning. I was used to the ever-present signs of crime, but I was yet to see anything which made me feel threatened. I liked Calloway the instant I walked through the eight-feet-tall electric gates. The driveway led to a small garage with the counsellors' office directly adjacent. An archway through the smooth white brick wall with the rusted metal words 'faith, hope, love, peace' hanging on it led to the garden. The main entrance to the house was through full-length double glass doors, found one step up to the terracotta tiled porch lining the front of the house. Laughter and splashes came from a swimming pool on the other side of the wall occupying a small area in front of the porch. It flanked a garden the size of a tennis court with long thick grass surrounded by high walls and mature tropical trees so tall that the house was completely secluded.

Crow arrived right on cue in the middle of the garden as I walked through the archway. He took large lunging strides to mark his territory and tempt the odd worm earth-side. I listened for the taunting pigeons, wondering whether I'd still hear their shrieking voices; none of them had shown up since Crow's ambush at Cedar Ridge. Would they try again here, or had my mind moved on? All indications from the counsellors were that the reason I came to secondary was to delve deeper, peeling the onion to find the core of who I really was. Four weeks of primary had peeled only the outer layers. I hadn't cried for three days and the thought of starting again in front of a new set of strangers was unpleasant.

Most of the tears which had already poured from me were laced with guilt. I'd been keeping them at bay for years. In England, I could just make it through to midday before I gave in to the craving for cocaine. Then I had the choice of calling the dealer or asking for help, but I enjoyed the slippery slope to hell, and everyone could come with me if they wanted. As detox gathered momentum, I let go of the tears. With the commitment to at least another two months of rehab I began to let go of more than a marriage. I took a decisive step towards paving my future path. The realisation that I was letting go of a life I'd lived for the last eighteen years brought a new grief for the loss of friendships with people who didn't need to let go of alcohol, but there was also a sense of relief. I was letting go of the unhealthy way I chose to enjoy myself with other people; I let go of the need to drink or take drugs to show I was one of them. I'd wasted enough time being the impostor.

Jimmy met me at the kitchen entrance to show me my room. A pretty brunette sat smoking on the porch with one of her long legs strewn over the arm of a garden chair and ample cleavage resting under a loose-fitting pink vest. All I knew about Calloway was that it was a therapeutic community where the 'real work' was done. It was where I'd have to learn to live with people again.

'Hey,' I said. My confidence surprised me.

'Hi there,' she replied, smiling and peering over the top of her designer shades.

I checked back at the pool, curious to see who was in there. Cassie sprang from underneath the water, her bikini top all but dragged off by the pull of the water. She bounced to a stand-still, adjusting her wet bikini over her breasts, and met my gaze, throwing me a frisky smile with her insanely blue eyes.

I hadn't seen as much female skin for a long time and while Cassie's game of chicken at the level crossing made me wonder about her state of mind, her body was clearly recovering very well from the ravages of her own brand of addiction. I felt an excitement rise in me usually reserved for the few seconds before I opened a wrap of cocaine, but this time it was a clean buzz. A hit from a girl I was drawing nearer to, disregarding the advice never to get distracted by a relationship in rehab and not for the first year of sobriety.

Jimmy and I were sharing rooms again. Ours was at the end of the long upstairs corridor with the girls' rooms at one end and the guys at the other. We were crammed into a room twelve feet by ten. Two sets of bunk beds occupied most of the space with a few feet to spare for changing. It was my worst nightmare. We had two roomies. Guy, a South African who worked on oil rigs: tall, well-built with fair hair and a smile so bright it instinctively made me smile whenever I saw it. And Darren, a seventeen-year-old from Germany, whose rock bottom consisted of being bundled into a sack, driven to the woods at night with a knife held to his testicles and left to find his own way home. I never heard anything more about his drug use and my inner critic attacked him with a suspicion he had come to Cape Town for a bit of a holiday to spend his father's cash on designer clothes and tanning lotion. Something about him agitated the shit out of me and when that happened we were told to look at ourselves for the same annoying trait. He was so fucking friendly and I wasn't used to people showing a genuine interest in me. When I'd finally managed to come to terms with his happiness, he started to teach himself to whistle for the first time. It was like a drunk blackbird singing all the wrong notes and it made me want to kill the fucker.

Most of us were trying to get clean together; there was an undeniable sense of safety in numbers. Any friction or issues between people living so closely together had to be dealt with in an adult manner, but I didn't know how to live with other people. I thought the deal was to get to know myself, and it was. The way to find 'me' was by returning to the land of the living again. No more isolation.

I soon found a way to adapt to living in such close quarters with other addicts. My life had been devoid of any kind of routine and the best way to fall asleep to muffle the snoring and other sounds of the bedroom was to make myself as tired as possible. My first experience of cross-addiction was an obsession with waking up earlier and earlier. I realised I had a problem when I started getting up at three-thirty for my solo walks to the gym at the Cavendish shopping mall.

As soon as I realised what kind of freedom secondary

treatment allowed us, I got walking. I embarked on sacred dawn walks in an effort to turn my body back into something resembling a temple. As I walked into the misty morning everyone in the house was still sleeping, including the members of the committee meetings in my head who usually convened later in the day once the therapy peeled off a few more layers of the impostor's skin. My mind was such a tranquil place in those early hours before nature's stillness was tainted by rush hour. The walks were a form of meditation for me, starting in dawn's half-light. The Cape Doctor was nowhere to be heard or felt, leaving the air free for birdsong. I didn't have to make conversation with anyone and I didn't feel threatened or alone. I started to like the person I was alone with.

Crow joined me on the way to the gym, keeping his distance, but staying where I could see him playing with the street lights. As they turned off with the new daylight, he turned them back on again, cawing with delight and swooping from post to post. The more time we spent in each other's vicinity, the more I began to sense where he was before I laid eyes on him. Every day he chose the same stretch of road which dipped steeply half a mile ahead of mc. I could almost see the top of some of the more distant lights. By my third walk I saw a familiar pattern emerging. Crow was turning the lights on in a zigzag starting with three lights in a straight line on the right side. He then darted across to the left side of the road, and back one, turning on the final three lights, swooping from post to post until a set of traffic lights ended the game. Regular as clockwork: every time I made the morning walk he was there in front of me, zigzagging away.

'What are you doing? Why won't you come and talk to me anymore?' I called out to him one morning.

'Caw, caw, caw,' he laughed, looping the loop and rolling acrobatically.

I knew there was no way I'd get myself all the way to Cape Town on the brink of extinction to be attacked on my way to the gym, and I felt a sense of self-preservation I could never remember having before. I experienced feelings of pure gratitude on my walks, for my body, which still functioned, and for being given the chance to get well in a warm and beautiful part of the world. I hadn't spent any time on my own for a month and those first morsels of independence were so delicious, like getting to know someone for the first time. The walks and exercise started to clear my head. Occasionally, I walked before the dawn disturbed the night. I loved being surrounded by the darkness; I felt so at home in the night. Like a blind man putting his faith in a new guide dog, I put trust in the force which sparkled away in the black air.

Main Road took me to within a mile of the end of suburbia and the start of Newlands Forest, which spread densely up the slopes of Newlands towards Devil's Peak and Table Mountain National Park. I usually arrived before the first mechanical noises were painted on the quiet morning canvas, leaving space for the sound to find me again, but this time it came to me instead of rebounding off the interior walls of my skull.

Such distractions were easy to pass off as lingering side effects of the dregs of psychosis, or I put it down to the thud of my feet on the tarmac echoing inside my ears. But if I stopped walking, the sound was still there. A deep hum filled the landscape to my left, with a rhythm to it, like the distant steps of King Kong trampling through the trees. I wanted to sprint into the forest to find the place where nature primed its jet engines, forgetting about the importance of returning to Calloway House in time for the community meeting. Those walks were the first time I heard the drumming so clearly.

The rush-hour hubbub swallowed it up by the time I left the gym, but I had no time to ponder something as yet invisible to me. Being late back to rehab would have consequences, like having to weed the garden or write an essay on punctuality, just as most things did if they weren't on my daily plan, like sex. While drink and drugs slowly became a thing of the past, my addictive tendencies still ran rife. Exercise released endorphins, filling me with powerful surges of invincibility, fuelling a new thirst – for Cassie's skin. Calloway House was all about managing my once unmanageable life. I was never late because I became obsessed with punctuality, determined to rise to everything expected of me. Anything the counsellors told me to do I'd do because, after all, they'd been to the edge as well and they knew how to find their way back.

When I returned to the house I found my place in the garden for my morning ritual. Every morning without fail for three months I picked up a plastic garden chair and planted myself at the end of the garden to read my daily contemplation, and do the same thing I did to send myself to sleep each night. I sent healing to my recovery. I'd been taught a way to send healing to myself with distance healing. Six months after my initiation into Reiki, my teacher imprinted three ancient symbols into the palm of my right hand making it a pen to draw keys of cosmic energy. I was rusty, barely remembering the words, lines and sequences, which needed a perfectionist's precision to ignite their power. I faltered at the beginning, but in the silence of the garden the shapes returned to me, as did the realisation that perfection wasn't important. It was my own truth which mattered. All I had to do was hold the intention and my hands found their way again, guided by the life-force which flowed through every living thing. The same life-giving spark that kept me breathing at night without me knowing. I called for help and it came to me. Closing my eyes, drawing the three symbols and holding myself in my praying hands, I believed that the universe went to work for my highest good. I had no idea what that was; I just trusted it was all working out for me.

'Are your ears burning, Aaron?' Jimmy said, as he sat on the grass next to me nervously twiddling his newly acquired grey key ring bearing the words, 'Clean and Serene for Thirty Days' written in gold.

'What's up?' I looked at him quizzically as I finished the Reiki by circling my right palm over the left three times and blowing any remnants of energy into the ether.

'Cassie's up, that's what – she's hot for you. Don't tell

me you didn't notice, dude.' Jimmy tapped my leg.

'Can't say I did, Jimmy,' I replied unconvincingly. 'I'm just focusing on my programme, mate.'

'You shag, you relapse. It's the first golden rule of rehab, Aaron. Doesn't mean everyone abides by it, not by any means. I like you, man. Reckon we should stay in touch when we get back to England, eh?'

'Yeah, I'd really like that. Cassie's cool, mate, there's definitely a vibe there. I can't say I'm not tempted, 'cos I am – and there's nothing back home stopping me.'

'This disease doesn't take prisoners, man. She'll fuck you up, look at her!'

'Yeah, look at her, she's hot,' I interrupted, irritated that Jimmy thought he knew what was best for me.

'Hey guys, community meeting!' Cassie called from the terrace, right on cue.

'Let's go, dude, gotta make the daily plans, remember – fail to plan, plan to fail!' Jimmy leapt to his feet like an electric shock.

I took a few more minutes to savour the magic of the garden. Crow guarded the border for bastard pigeons. His loud, frequent caws translated the delight he had for the chase as the pigeons tested his flying skills. He swooped and turned sharply, catching one with his feet and throwing it into trees, clearing the space for me to pray and connect with the earth and heavens before approaching the day's onion peeling. The pigeons were a stubborn blight on my serenity. The last week of rock-bottom left my head exposed for them to imprint their madness on me. It clung like a parasite, blighting my brain. Thankfully, something new arrived in the garden to lift my spirits.

The counsellors said they'd never seen an eagle owl in the garden before. It was enormous at over half a metre tall. The surrounding trees were so high that I couldn't see the sky without cricking my neck backwards at an awkward angle. It took me a while to find him; when I did, his eyes beamed straight at me, their wise stare as old as the stars themselves. Before I took my place each morning on a patch of sunshine-bathed grass, I acknowledged the owl and Crow.

My recovery was creating a lot of interest. As each new day cleaned out the cobwebs, banished the skeletons and covered me with new skin, the spirit world beckoned.

NINE

After two weeks of regular visits to the gym, my body began to grow some muscle again and the first hint of self-confidence in my appearance returned. I could, at last, look at myself in the mirror with pride instead of disgust, and an element of interest as someone new started to emerge in front of my eyes with each scrutinising look at my reflection. The gym gave me a chance to escape the sometimes claustrophobic rehab environment; Calloway House was full to the brim.

I rewarded myself with a new pair of swimming shorts and decided to brave the swimming pool for the first time. At the end of a sweltering day I joined Jimmy, Cassie and Guy in the pool. We were drained from our written work. As if it weren't hard enough to process the emotions, we also had to write a minimum of one thousand words every day.

'Blimey, Aaron, check out your guns!' Jimmy yelled as I threw down my towel.

'No pain, no gain,' I replied. My workouts were intense. Still obsessed with pushing my body to its limits, I loved searching for excruciating muscle-burn, which left me grimacing and yelping in pain. The cigarette burns healed, but I found something else to replace the sting on my skin.

I granted myself a glance at Cassie's small yet perfectly formed arse as she lay on the air bed. Her buttocks were escaping from a small pink bikini. She looked so inviting as the silver sun danced on the ripples surrounding her, turning droplets of water into pearls of light as the hot tanned skin of her thighs sipped them in. I met her eyes, briefly, before I shyly duck-dived under the water. I returned for a second look at her now smiling face as the water lapped up the sexual charge between us. We floated our way round the small oasis without conversation, just the occasional sigh and intimate laugh of gratitude to our higher powers. I began to allow myself bursts of happiness. After all the badness, I welcomed the goodness life now presented. Guy was the first to break the silence.

'Where'd ya get that tattoo, man? What does the wing mean?' he said.

I guessed he was referring to something on Jimmy or Cassie I hadn't seen, but none of them answered. I looked at Guy; he was looking at me.

'What are you talking about, mate?' I said.

'The tattoo… on your back,' he said.

'It's not a tattoo,' I replied.

'Come on, tell us what it means,' Cassie asked.

'I just told you, it's not a tattoo.'

'Everyone's got a story behind their tattoo, haven't they, bud?' Jimmy said, pogoing in the shallow end. 'What's yours? It looks cool, anyway.'

'Mmmm, really cool.' Cassie sighed, presumably at the thought of the pain from the tattoo gun.

'Let's go, spill the beans, buddy,' Guy said.

I reached over my right shoulder to feel the skin. My fingertips felt the patch of raised skin. I nearly went for the sunburn story. Jimmy and I were having a tanning competition. Tanorexia was a new addiction; we didn't give a shit. We were in Cape Town for the summer so we relentlessly milked serotonin from the sun. I rubbed my left hand to feel the lower patch of skin on the same side. No one had noticed it for years. The so-called tattooing experience was hidden from me, or maybe I was hiding from it. I tuned out of the conversation and slipped into my quiet zone, incubated, safe. I sifted through the flash-frames of memory. Cassie approached me in the shallow end while I zoned out. The sound of her breath brought me back.

'Please let me see, Aaron,' she said, checking for the prying eyes of a counsellor.

'Okay,' I replied. Cassie could do anything she wanted. Her breathing quickened and reverberated with the sound of her racing heartbeat, she was so close. Water from her face dripped onto my shoulder. The water-softened tips of her fingers rubbed over the rough, scarred skin on my back. At first back and forth, then in circles, before playfully making figure-of-eights.

'Beautiful,' she said, pressing her lips against the scar, flicking a switch inside me. I spun round to face her, wanting only to grab a fistful of her hair and pull her head back to taste her tongue. Jimmy and Guy were staring at me, transfixed and slobbering. I silently stepped out of the pool, moving in front of the full-length window, my arm arched behind my back to touch the shape. My life was littered with accidents and injuries, from childhood misdemeanours to adult drunken foolery. I'd managed to place all but the one that had actually killed me.

'Get a room!' Jimmy said, pogoing faster.

'Good idea,' I whispered, moving closer to the window, my breathing made shallower by the unbearable sexual tension and the shock of seeing what I'd always wanted to stay blind to.

'Lightning… I was struck by lightning. It's not a tattoo, it's a burn scar.'

'Fuuuuuck!' Cassie said. Jimmy and Guy looked like they'd seen a ghost. Not so far from the truth. Suddenly I needed space from them; I was overcome with light-headedness, and my legs were about to give way.

'Time out,' I said, making a 'T' with my hands. I walked into my garden shell, squinting away from the sunlight as the images I normally used alcohol to escape from flashed into my head. I heard Cassie's light footsteps following me.

'You okay, Aaron?' she said, sitting next to me on the grass with a towel wrapped round her body.

'Yep, I just need to try and process this shit. It's been festering away inside me.'

'What happened to you? That's one freaky-looking scar.' Cassie crossed her arms and ran her fingers over the criss-cross scars on her shoulders.

'I'm not entirely sure. Sometime in the early nineties, I can't remember what year, I went to the East Coast of Canada to see a group of friends. They were like family to me. It must've been my fourth or fifth trip out there. I say 'sometime' because the good times all blurred into one. Hanging out in lake cabins, camping in the Gatineau Hills and road trips to some of the best rock concerts; the gigs were frickin' awesome! I never recalled much about that last trip though. Just before I came to Cape Town I opened an email from a close friend out there asking why I never came to see her. The only explanation I have is a mixture of truth and speculation, which I blamed on the vast amounts of LSD we were doing. I nearly sat on a baby at the Grateful Dead concert in Buffalo before the dad gently guided me to the next seat along. The lightning strike happened sometime after we'd seen Crosby, Stills and Nash in Vermont, New England. I still have the ticket and a collection of really weird memories which come back to me in dreams or when I'm out on my own walking anywhere in the woods. The lightning was just the climax of years of close shaves with fire; most of the burns happened when I was tripping. They gradually got worse. If there was a fire burning in a campsite at a festival I'd just stay there and let my soul dance with the flames. I'd hallucinate huge fires burning on hillsides miles off in the distance and just head off on my own to find the flames, which leads me to my LSD party trip. I went missing every time I tripped, waking up on deserted hillsides frazzled and lost. At the CSN concert we'd all been taking some beautiful acid with Mick Jagger lips on them, but I took a few more. That's what this disease is, eh? The disease of more! I remember sitting on the hill, a natural amphitheatre, we were all passing weed, hugging and watching the band. It was the summer equinox, the moon partially eclipsed. It started out as one of the most beautiful, crazy nights of my life. People started falling down the hill. I couldn't tell if they were doing it for fun or were just too out of it to dance on a ski slope, but one after the other they avalanched down. That was the last thing I remember before waking up in hospital. Well, nearly the last thing. They found me two days later at the foot of a giant hollowed-out redwood still smouldering after a lightning strike. The sap acted as a super-conductor and just shot the electricity down the tree. They said I'd been leaning against it when it hit. I was naked. I'd been eating wild berries and leaves. The papers called me the 'British Sasquatch'. I spent weeks on my stomach with one of those tents over my back to let the burns heal.'

'What about the wings, Aaron?' Cassie asked, shuffling closer, letting her towel fall down. She looked damn good in pink as the breeze teased her nipples out of hiding. I tried not to let her pollute my recovery, but gave way easily to the image of my hand slipping into her wet bikini. The thought of dirty sex when I was clean became very attractive. I justified my intentions by presuming other clients were messing around, especially when we lived in such close quarters to each other. The roller-coaster ride of emotions continued, with guilt and anger overflowing into tearfulness whenever group or one-to-one therapy took place. But the highs were beginning to out-number the lows, and I began to see Cassie as a welcome distraction from the divorce. Maybe I could have some fun in rehab without relapsing; maybe that rule didn't apply to me.

'I don't know what the wings are about, Cassie. I mean, I'm beginning to get an idea, but everything's opening up so quickly, like I'm coming out of hibernation. Let's change the subject,' I said. We looked at each other, exchanging mischievous smiles. I found her conflicting appearance so intriguing. She had it all, with her slinky figure, super-model elfin looks and a voice to lull the angels down from heaven with. Yet her skin and psyche were permanently marked by self-mutilation. I found her so interesting because she reflected me; I was no different. I tried to hold my trembling hand still in front of me and wondered if my body would ever fully recover. As the fog cleared I began to see how similar I was to everyone at Calloway House.

'What do you do down here in the mornings?' Cassie said, her toes tapping on my foot.

'Reiki, I'm sending Reiki to myself and my recovery. I fall asleep every night sending healing to myself, I've only got one recovery in me.'

'What's Reiki?'

'It's a Japanese word. Rei means universal. Ki means life-force, same as chi in Chinese, or prana in Sanskrit. It's the energy that keeps your heart beating and your lungs breathing when you're asleep. Reiki is that spark that makes you want to take your next breath. It has its own intuition, going to where it's needed most, working on physical, mental, emotional and spiritual levels; it's so deeply cleansing and detoxifying. You can treat people hands-on with level one Reiki, or send it to people and situations with level two.'

'How do you do the hands-on treatment?' Cassie said.

'Like this. Reiki on, Reiki off.' I placed the palm of my hand on the small of her back for a few seconds and removed it. 'There are twelve hand positions, starting on the head and then working down the front and back of the body. Most people feel some heat or feel tingling; it's very relaxing.'

'Can I have some, please,' Cassie said.

The thought of having such open access to Cassie's body was exhilarating, but Reiki was a sacred, healing art, and not to be used immorally. I'd only treated friends and family, so there was never any question of eroticism clouding my healing intentions, but that was then. I wasn't sure how stable my moral fibre was anymore and right then, I didn't care.

'Sure, that'd be cool. Why don't you meet me in the group therapy room tomorrow morning. It'll need to be early before anyone wakes up: say, five o'clock. I'll lay some sofa cushions on the floor for you?'

'Lovely, see you at dinner,' Cassie said in a husky voice. She stood up, using my shoulder for leverage, and stole one more stroke of my lightning scar before leaving me in the garden.

Rehab wasn't supposed to be like this, or was it? After missing last summer cooped up with my demons, I found baking in the sun the perfect remedy and spent the rest of the day in the garden with owl, Crow, and the wind cooling my skin. Balanced perfectly with nature, waves of pure happiness caressed me as I rested on the soft green carpet of the earth. Maybe rehab was supposed to be like this. I found myself smiling that evening for no apparent reason, just because I felt at ease with where I was, what I was doing, and who I was doing it with.

The house was full to the brim with twenty-four recovering addicts trying to find a way back. At most, a third of us would make it and stay clean for the rest of our lives. A third would relapse but find the way back to rehab to try again, and a third wouldn't make it at all. Quite which ratio I fitted into wasn't definite, but each new day clean cemented my path to recovery. It was easy to deny that Cassie posed a risk to the integrity of that path; she was a gift from my higher power and I looked forward to opening the present.

She arrived in the group therapy room half asleep with bed-head hair and shut the door behind her, as quiet as a mouse.

'Where do you want me?' she asked, standing by the door in hipster gym shorts and a cropped cotton vest which left her collarbones protruding.

'Come and lie here. Do you want a blanket?' I said, holding out a throw from the sofa.

'No, your hands can keep me warm,' Cassie said, lying in front of me. Her head rested on a pillow between my legs as I sat astride the makeshift bed which consisted of three large square cushions. She stretched her arms above her head and yawned, raising her vest nipple-height in the process, exposing the lower half of her breasts. Her hands softly cupped my face before she lowered them, lightly tugging her shorts down to expose her pelvis.

I lit a candle, placed one hand over her left eye and drew the Reiki symbols over her face before softly covering both her eyes. Cassie's breaths deepened, and the diamond in her belly-button piercing sparkled in the candle light at the peak of her inhalations. My hands tingled wildly with energy, gradually heating up to scalding levels which felt as if they should be burning her eyes from their sockets – but for all its sensation of heat, Reiki never raised the temperature. It was just the energy's way of working. I closed my eyes onto a screen of golden light, sensing the energy travelling through the top of my head to my heart and down my arms to the chakras in my palms, and then into Cassie's every being.

The freshness of the first tears as they trickled down her cheeks distracted me. The clock had moved on ten minutes in what felt like the blink of an eye; my hands were drawn as if magnetised to her face as the energy quickened, satisfying her mind, body and soul's thirst for healing. I moved my hands to her temples, exposing her eyes, scrunched with emotion, and I reached for a tissue to dry her eyes before placing both hands in the next position. The caring dab of the tissue prompted more release. The quivering of her lips brought forth gentle sobbing; her stomach muscles tensed and relaxed as she poured out the pain, leaving a space for loving energy to find her. I moved my hands under the base of her skull, cradling her head, creating a channel for the warm pulsating Reiki to radiate into her. Cassie covered her face with her hands, delicately wiping the tears from her face as her spirit calmed. She took a long breath, blowing through her lips on the exhale as the emotional roller-coaster came to an end.

'Move your hands down, Aaron,' she whispered, lightly flicking the diamond piercing back and forth with the ring finger of her right hand. The heat of the day was yet to stir, but beads of sweat appeared on my brow.

I rested her head on the cushion and shuffled to her side, never letting my hands leave her body to keep the connection we'd created. Her breathing quickened as one hand touched her shoulder, then her forearm, and the other rested on her leg as I shuffled into position, finally placing both palms on her ribcage, exposed by her flimsy vest. She took a deep breath, expanding her ribcage to meet my hands as they rested inches from her breasts. I was losing control of any ethical principles which spiritual healing stood for, and surrendering to the lust laid out before me. She was mine for the taking: a just reward for making it this far in recovery.

After five minutes I moved my hands lower towards their prize and their heat reached sun-like temperatures. Cassie kept her eyes closed, preferring the kinkiness of her self-imposed blindfold. She bit her bottom lip as my hands rested below her piercing, carelessly flicking it back and forth with my thumb on the way down; she whimpered, tilting her neck back, and simultaneously raised her arms above her head in total submission. Her shorts slipped lower over the perfect hills of her pelvic bones. My breathing synchronised with hers, and my head slumped lower as her force-field pulled me closer into her, alternating between the sweetness of her tongue and her excited nipples. She reached down to guide my right hand inside her; raising and lowering her torso. Slowly at first, but then with an urgency, purring and writhing like a cat in heaven with every stroke. She took control of my hand for the finale, determined not to miss the gloriousness of her orgasm which came with the eureka-scream of someone finding the Holy Grail. She was gone, lost in the bliss, but her scream made stirrings in the house.

'What the fuck was that?' a male voice said from the upstairs balcony, followed by a few frantic footsteps thumping on the ceiling, and then nothing. The house fell silent again.

'Your turn,' Cassie said, smiling like an out-of-breath Cheshire cat.

Footsteps came from above again, this time to the stairs and down to the kitchen where the noise of crockery and a boiling kettle distracted Cassie from the very important task in hand, and destroyed my proud wood. Unfortunately the only thing Cassie swallowed was the glass of water I'd left next to her before we scampered out of the room to avoid the first arrivals for breakfast in the adjacent kitchen.

My head was in the clouds for the rest of the day, wondering when I'd get another chance to be alone with Cassie. I walked out of the gates to the Seven Eleven to replenish my cigarette supply, licking my lips to taste any remnants of Cassie's orange lip balm. The noon heat and breeze combined to waft the sweet smell of marijuana plants over the highly fortified wall of a neighbouring house. I closed my eyes to savour the celestial perfume as it found the few parts of my nostrils which hadn't been destroyed by cocaine. The long inhalation stopped me in my tracks. I imagined being consumed by a cloud of weed-infused smoke and then passing the joint to a naked Cassie and snorting a circle of cocaine from the circumference of her pierced tanned belly-button.

The walk took me past the small barbers Jimmy had visited to get his hair cut. Male pattern baldness and a chemical diet had left a hairstyle the shape of a toilet seat on my head. To stop for a number one clip would've been unplanned and a deviation with consequences which didn't matter to me. I smoked my fresh Marlboro in the two minutes it took to get from the store to the barbers and stepped inside.

A tall, tattooed, pony-tailed man motioned me towards a leather chair with sturdy arm rests. Led Zeppelin played from an old-fashioned stacking system stereo with a vertical compact disc loader which showed the disc rotating. The smell of fresh coffee filled the room as it gurgled into a percolator. I faced myself in the mirror, ready for the shave. Crow arrived in the reflection behind me, balancing on the sports bar's picket fence across the street. He looked agitated, constantly adjusting his wings and firing splinters in every direction as he attacked the fence with his black pickaxe of a beak.

'Wanna coffee?' the barber said, standing behind me. He reached his head to tighten the band on his ponytail, exposing needle marks on the soft skin of his forearms.

'No thanks, just a number one all over,' I replied, watching him oil the blades. I felt a brief sense of reassurance that another addict was about to shave my head and assist in my ongoing personal transformation, until I noticed the lack of life behind his eyes: a look I'd seen before in my own eyes. I wanted to say 'Forget it!' and peg it back to rehab, but I wasn't sure when I'd have the balls to shave my head again.

'What's an English accent doing in Claremont? It's not much of a holiday destination,' he said. The clippers fired into action with a loud 'clap'! He paused, waiting for me to tell him what he already knew.

'I'm in rehab at Calloway House,' I said unashamedly.

'Huh, another one. Why are ya' comin' over here to

our rehabs?' The clippers pressed firmly into the base of my skull and zoomed up the back of my head. I watched more of the old me fall away to the floor.

'It's cheaper for a start. One month's treatment here costs the same as one week in the UK,' I said. The buzz of the clippers filled my ears as his expert strokes moved in smooth curves to the side of my head, exposing the new me.

'Guess that means you won't be wanting any of this, then.' He stopped the clippers and picked up a small green porcelain bowl with a golden Chinese dragon dancing around its circumference. He lifted the lid and pushed the bowl under my nose. It was filled with wraps of cocaine and small bundles of grass. My heart sprinted to full-speed as the thought of going on a bender with Cassie flashed into my head. Just one night in a hotel room: what harm could it do? My self-will ran riot like a rodeo bull busting through the gates, intent on causing as much chaos as possible.

'Caw!' Crow hopped madly, trashing empty tables behind me. 'Caw!' Glasses and ashtrays smashed to the floor. The barber, oblivious to the mayhem, hummed along to Stairway to Heaven and placed the bowl of drugs next to the sink in front of me. He picked up the clippers to make the tidying touches to my head, just as Crow flew headlong into the window. His head butted the huge pane of glass as the rock classic reached its crescendo, muffling his attack. Unshaken, he flew away, circling the roof of the sports bar, screaming 'Caw! Caw!' before returning for another kamikaze run. His head hit the window as the song finished. I caught the fury in his eyes as he hovered briefly before disappearing. The bang of Crow's head twitched the barber's heroin-frayed nerves.

'Fuck it,' he said, reaching for a tissue and handing it to me. The tickle of blood surprised me as it ran down my forehead. I looked at the dragon bowl, all craving for sex and drugs shattered by the rock and roll of Crow's disdain. All I saw was a bowl full of hell and panic.

'Keep that shit away from me,' I said, throwing fifty rand in the sink and tearing the towel from my neck to find Crow. He was nowhere to be seen. I walked back to Calloway House taking solace in the new sensory experience of rubbing my scalp. I was shaken by the filth of the experience, but the head-shave helped me take one more step away from the impostor I hated so much.

'Crow! Crow!' I shouted. And then I stopped still, suddenly aware of the spectacle I was making of myself and the strength of my attachment to him. I looked to the lamp posts for his magic trick, or for pigeons flying for their lives, but all was quiet.

Jimmy was waiting outside the electric gate; his rapid back-and-forth sentry walk skidded to a halt when he saw me approaching. His smile turned to sombreness when he saw my shaved head.

'Shit, Aaron, you look like Bruce Willis! You've seen that junkie barber, haven't you?'

'Yep, fucker tried to sell me Charlie and weed.'

'Don't go changing, buddy, you're doing so well. You

looked like a rabbit caught in the headlights when I met you at Cedar Ridge. Look at you now!' Jimmy put a friendly hand on my shoulder. 'Cape Town is a long way to come for a relapse. Don't forget, we'll need each other when we get home.'

'No shit, Sherlock,' I smiled. Jimmy was right, the barber was just the first in a long line of temptations waiting for me back in England, but my story was changing. I'd escaped the lion's den as a slave, soon to return with a new strength, ready to do battle as a gladiator, 'Do you know when you're going home yet?'

'One more month here, then back to the shit storm. I'd stay forever if it weren't for my kids; the only way I can sort out custody is with the court. The heavies threatening my friends and family have been paid off. Amazing, really. My wife asked a philanthropist friend of ours to pay the half-a-million, which he did, but he's told me never to contact him again.'

'Funny how the people we hurt can be the ones who save us in the end, isn't it? I may never have known about Cape Town if my sister hadn't suggested it,' I said as we walked through the gliding gate towards the group therapy room for our afternoon session.

'Yep, damn right, life is full of surprises,' Jimmy said, taking his place in the circle of empty chairs. His knees started bouncing like a springboard missing its recently departed diver.

I was clucking for the session to start so I could share what had happened at the barbers, to stop it festering away inside me.

'Secrets keep you sick,' Jimmy whispered.

'I know. Shut up, wise guy.'

The other community members took their seats, except Cassie. I spent the session waiting for her long legs to walk through the door, and for the first time I didn't cry. The Serenity Prayer was working. From somewhere new within me I'd found the strength to walk away from the barbers. But I still wanted more of Cassie; I'd conjured up an ever-increasing list of things I wanted to do to her during her next Reiki treatment. That was a secret I wasn't prepared to let go of just yet.

'Thanks for sharing that, Aaron. Anything else you need to share with the group?' the counsellor said, looking at me from behind the tobacco-blackened circles around her eyes.

'No... thank you.'

'Sure?'

'Yep,' I said, squirming from the sudden nausea hitting me with the realisation that she knew about my morning escapade with Cassie.

'Hmm, strange, Cassie didn't say the same thing in her one-to-one earlier. She's waiting in the drive to say goodbye. Session over,' the bitch said, wobbling her turkey-gizzard chin with a pen.

The nausea increased. I left the room quickly to find Cassie standing by a taxi.

'I'm sorry, Aaron, it just came out. Secrets keep you sick anyway,' she said, forcing a smile.

'Shit, I'm sick of hearing that bollocks. I know you're right though. Guess you blinded me with your light a little,' I said, stopping her tear in its tracks with my fingertip before sampling its salty taste on my tongue.

'The counsellor told my parents straight away. They're moving me to a rehab in Hout Bay. Mum said she wouldn't have me back until the counsellors said I was ready. Thing is, the counsellors don't get it that my parents are half the problem,' she replied, pushing her tits against my chest. She licked one of my tears from my cheek with her tongue. 'And you're the other half; I can't get enough of you. See ya round, Aaron,' she said, synchronizing a gentle squeeze of my crotch with the planting of a soft kiss on my lips. Her hand pushed inside my pocket, further than needed, to leave me a piece of paper with her phone number on it. And she was gone. Departing with a physicality that defined our friendship more than any of the few spoken words we'd exchanged could.

Crow kept out of sight, but his loud calls of delight circled the rehab as he flew victory rolls, celebrating Cassie's departure.

TEN

I felt strong and clearheaded the next morning. There was a sharpness in the air. Or perhaps it was in me. So sharp, it reminded me of the first escalation in my senses after taking acid. As if reality had been altered, somehow, but I felt so energised and positive. I knew all I had to do was to keep doing what I was doing – turning up for community group on time; doing my chores around the house; talking to the counsellors in my one-on-ones to put the pieces back together and sitting in the garden next to a swimming pool writing the boring, monotonous, healing step-work.

Crow lit the lights in his usual pattern. The dots joined up, each light haloed by the blurring morning mist helping me to see the pattern he'd been drawing with new clarity. The light-bulb moment was sublime. Crow's flight path of illumination showed me the classic zigzag lightning strike. I stopped to touch the outskirts of my burn scar and walked the hundred or so yards between the last two lamp posts, where he waited, still refusing to talk to me, unskilled in the classic recovery technique of letting go of resentments. He stretched his neck as far as his body would allow, calling the loudest 'caw!' I'd ever heard into the still dawn air. The response came almost immediately as the hum of the drum beat lulled me.

'Boom-boom! Boom-boom!'

I walked to its rhythm. Each footstep timed with Mother's beating heart. I paused at the crossroads. No traffic rumble, no people: all banished for this moment. The drumming stopped for a few seconds. Then it started again, louder, and my body pulsed with energy.

A left turn would take me on a detour away from the gym to Newlands Forest, but to do so meant risking being late back for the morning community meeting and deviating from my daily plan would have definite consequences from the counsellors. There was logic in the Calloway House rules. My life had become unmanageable, partly through impulsive decision-making, and here I was again on the brink of pressing the 'fuck it' button to see what Mother wanted. I didn't think I could risk saying I'd ditched the gym because I'd heard drumming calling me to the forest. I stood there, weighing up the pros and cons of each direction, closing my eyes to bring in the Serenity Prayer for guidance, and in the silence induced by 'the wisdom to know the difference' the answer came to me in a wave of fear. Until now I'd done everything by the book – granted, some of it included the Kama Sutra. But to the best of my ability, I'd given my will and my life to the twelve-step programme and had asked for a new way to live. The detour would tell everyone that, after only two months of sobriety, I knew best – but I didn't. I felt like a baby on reins. They'd lengthened the reins a little to let me get to the gym as a show of trust in my recovery, and in me. I could disrespect that and loosen the chains on the gates of hell. I had no idea where that complacent swerve would lead to – just like I had no idea what would happen if I drank again. Sure, it could be a slow burner, nothing happening for a week or so. I'd try to control alcohol, and before too long end up in jail, a straitjacket or six feet under. Or it would be a quick, hideous relapse, waking in the gutter with the shit kicked out of me. When I looked at it like that, there was no dilemma; all impulsiveness dissolved. I kept to the path and the plan.

As I passed the sliding gates of Calloway House on my return from the gym session, I went straight to the garden to connect with the life-force growing in and around me. While I knew I'd made the right decision, the pull of Newlands Forest clouded my mind with its presence. Scenes of dense forest constantly appeared in my mind. I could distract myself momentarily by focusing on the owl or something mundane like my hand, but the visions remained. My surroundings developed a transparency, like a thin veil filtering messages through to me.

With the transparency came a chain of events which screamed synchronicity at me. The first event had happened that day when one of the counsellors, Troy, came into breakfast to tell us about a change of programme for the day. I liked Troy a lot. He had a quiet voice, but his passion for recovery and the new life it offered all of us was so inspiring. I also liked him because we bore the same marks – he had burn scars on his face and neck – and because of the first words I ever heard him say when he walked into the kitchen for my first community group.

'You know what I did yesterday morning, guys?' Everyone held their breath. 'I took a drive over Chapman's Peak. Ah, the sun just started to climb above the sea. I pulled over before I got to Camps Bay and filled my clean lungs with salty sea air and the only thing I had to think about was how flat the sea was. I hadn't a care in the world. My head was quiet and I just listened to the wind for a while. I felt so free!' Troy beamed a smile of hope over us all from the end of the table. I wanted a piece of that serenity. I was in awe of him.

That morning Troy had come in from the counsellors' office adjoining the kitchen. 'Guys, we're gonna give you a free session this morning. You need to choose between staying at Calloway, or going to Camps Bay or Newlands Forest for three hours, and then back for lunch.'

My stomach flipped with excitement at the news. The surprise of a free morning lifted the low morale in the house. Occasionally the group energy became stagnant as people got stuck in their problems, unable to see the solution staring them in the face. No one tried to hide their excitement. The room whooped and hollered, and most of the group sprinted for their beach gear – except me.

A walk in the woods wouldn't normally raise my adrenalin. Troy frequently described himself as being 'so excited!' for us in the hope we'd grasp recovery and 'another chance' at life. Right then I was as excited as a dog being shown the lead for its first walk of the day. Troy's eyes caught mine as, along with the rest of the group, I headed for the waiting transit vans. He smiled at me. The driver took the long route through the city to Camps Bay to drop off the beach gang. This gave me my first broadside of Table Mountain as we took the motorway past the business district, and then into Sea Point. We sang along to Bob Marley's 'Redemption Song'. His music had become anthems for us: a soundtrack for a unique, opportune time of my life. Even with the music playing I still heard the mountain, and I still felt Mother calling me.

The rhythm was gone but her deep hum lifted my eyes towards her magnetic mass. I traced the slopes of the national park, catching the stripes of a zebra as it darted for cover. I looked up at the long flat table-top, cutting into the light-blue sky. No cable car ran the near-vertical path to the station on the right tip. The Cape Doctor poured a medicinal layer of thick white cloud over the lip of the mountain. It was the most powerful image of nature I'd ever seen as Mother's cauldron cooked the healing mists, cascading it over her troubled city.

I wasn't a stranger to roaming the woods. A trip to The Gambia to get over my first broken heart had introduced me to the finest African weed – and, more importantly, to drumming! I'd spent three weeks with an African drum maker and owner of the Fish Eagle Hotel, in a small town on the outskirts of Fajara. Amar was a stocky fisherman made of bone and hard muscle. His hands were weathered from pulling in the lines as he trawled for barracuda in the mangroves of the River Gambia; his biceps were big enough to strangle an anaconda. We spent most of our days smoking, drumming, and getting lost in the mangroves, occasionally mooring onto small islands inhabited by sole giant baobab trees. Eagles launched themselves from dead trees overhanging the river, plucking fish from the water so close to our small boat that I could hear their talons tearing into the water.

'That was just for you,' Amar would say. He told me stories in a hushed voice about the black magic of the mangroves. I had no reason to disbelieve a man who looked as if he could kill anyone with his bare hands, yet clearly he feared Africa's unseen juju.

'You know, mate,' he said early one morning as we left the mooring in town, 'there's a superstition here that if you see a monkey wave at you, it's going to bring you bad luck that day, and right over there I saw a monkey wave at me once. Sure enough on our way home we saw a man fishing from that footbridge we're going to pass under. I caught his line, and you know what, mate, he turned out to be the chief of police. He confiscated my lines and a bag of weed hidden inside a freshly caught fish.'

I didn't question his respect for the juju of the area. In

fact I liked the idea of people respecting magic. I could feel it when we stopped for lunch on one of the small islands to cast a rod and smoke. After three weeks of drumming with Amar, my hands had grown calluses from repeatedly slamming against the coconut wood rim to perfect the gunshot slap. Evening Muslim prayer time brought the old man from next door out to stand on the cliff-edge, meditating with the setting sun on one side and the rising moon on the other.

On my first walk to the local supermarket at a crossroads not more than a few hundred yards away from the guest house, I returned laden with two packed plastic bags of shopping, but I took the wrong turn and didn't realise my error until the handles were digging into my skin. As I turned around to see where I'd gone wrong, I heard the chatter of children finishing school for the day across the dusty red road. The teacher was at the gate ushering them out so I crossed to ask him where my hotel was. Instead of telling me, he walked me all the way back to the guest house with the whole school in tow. The children found me a very amusing spectacle with toilet rolls and crisp packets poking out of the bags: a white man lost in Africa. Soon after my return to England, I began working with disabled children in their schools, and somehow I knew the universe had told me that this was my vocation, by sending a happy gang of African children to guide me back safely.

As soon as I got home I was drawn to the local woods with marijuana and my drum. I spent as much of my spare time there as possible. I especially loved the night time. The car parks emptied as dusk approached. It wasn't really a place to be on your own, but I felt more life stir around me in the darkness of the forest. During the day I'd perch myself on a fallen tree at the edge of the ridge overlooking the strawberry fields of the farm below and let my stare drift miles into the distance. Sometimes I'd hear the birds freaking out as the drum reverberated off the tree trunks, or dog-walkers would call over, 'do you have to do that?' but mostly my drumming was met with appreciation and compliments. In summer the heat tightened the goat skin, singing in unison with the base which came as my palm hit the centre of the drum. My devotion to the drum began to pay off; with less need to focus on what I was doing with my hands, I found trance-like states where my hands flowed effortlessly to a rhythm coming from both inside and all around me. My lungs forgot about the need for air. I breathed rhythm.

Things were different at night though. I couldn't see anything around me, just heard the occasional animal foraging through the undergrowth. I'd focus on the flames of my fire or close my eyes and let the darkness cover me. I felt a sense of belonging to the forest. It comforted me and kept me safe from the confusing world that lay beyond the boundaries of the trees, and I felt appreciation from the trees and animals, and from the darkness itself. Every time I locked my car and left the street lights of the car park behind me to walk into the dark forest, I breathed a sigh of relief, and the air loosened around me as I let the darkness in. I felt so at home.

When we arrived at Newlands Forest car park I waited for the other hikers to pick their routes before leaving. I wanted to be on my own in the forest with no chance of someone tagging along with me. I'd learnt to be assertive for the first time in my life, but I hadn't perfected the art by a long way, and usually I ended up offending the other person, which helped me learn another new skill – apologising, and meaning it. I walked the main path out of the car park that would eventually lead me to the top of the mountain, but I didn't have the time or inclination to go there… yet. I wasn't ready for whatever was up there waiting for me. The Mother of all rocks called for me. My ascent would be inevitable, be it by foot or cable car – when? That was the only question.

I searched for a part of the forest where the trees and plants hadn't been disturbed by a human presence for years. Sure, they'd say I was isolating myself, and I was. I loved isolation. I just wanted to be alone as I'd been years ago after my return from The Gambia, but I wanted to experience it with a clean buzz. I was curious to know if I could recreate anything close to my flight with Crow in England without my mind being thick with psychosis. I could feel a new craving to be away from the metal and concrete of society. I wanted to rest on Mother's earth, my skin to hers.

I looked behind me; the path was clear and the air bristled with insect chatter. I stepped off the path, ducking and threading my way through the trees, but as soon as I put one foot inside the first row of trees, the forest stopped, listening. Every animal suddenly felt my presence enter their domain. I contemplated my next step with the apprehension of a soldier negotiating a minefield. I held my breath and took one more step, then another and another before the forest started talking again. The earth was soft with pine needles, lit up in a patchwork of sunrays fortunate enough to find a space through the thick canopy. The air was full of their sweet, musty scent, calming me, briefly distracting me from realising that Crow was nowhere to be seen or heard. I paused in my stride to listen, but there was no distant caw or rustling of branches above me, no sense of him anywhere. I walked on, occasionally looking back to see the path gradually disappearing from view. Pine trees huddled all around, seducing me further away from the path, intoxicating me with their sweet, heady aroma. A drunken giddiness overcame me. I stopped, closed my eyes and turned in circles with my arms outstretched. Light filled my eyes; the aroma of pine turned to the smell of burning sage. I inhaled deeply to take the sacred smell as far inside my lungs as possible. My ecstasy turned to agony as the scar on my back burned like hell. I ripped off my shirt, running and screaming in agony as I flailed my arms hopelessly to extinguish the invisible flames; trees lacerated my skin as their branches lunged for me. I'd lost all sense of direction, all knowledge of the path's location reduced to guesswork. A hollowed tree stump stood in front of me, ten feet tall, severed. A curved opening formed a grand wooden chair, throne-like, bathed in a shaft of sunlight. I moved closer, removing the rest of my clothes as my eyesight focused in high-definition, and my hearing picked up every forest-floor rustle and shimmer of leaf in the wind. A natural high lifted my spirit. The initial flashes of light scared the shit out of me. Convinced I was suffering a brain haemorrhage as final payback, I fell to my knees in front of the tree. My hands gripped the charred ridge of the seat. I pulled myself up, sweat pouring from my brow. I braced myself, white-knuckled on the blackened wood, with my back cradled by the softened light-brown interior of the bark as the trauma from New England hit me like a freight train.

At first, his dark Indian face appeared slowly from the darkened recesses of the forest. He waited until the birds, freaked by his presence, left the area en masse, screeching in panic. As the silence settled, he walked towards me, his body wrapped in a large rust-coloured blanket patterned with green leaves which brushed his bare feet. With each footstep the sound of small bones wrapped round his ankles punctuated the stillness. The smell of burning white sage grew stronger as he came closer, pausing momentarily, seeming uncertain that he could believe what he was seeing. A faint smile appeared on his serious face, and he raised his eyebrows like someone surprised at a chance meeting with a long-lost friend.

All sense of my physical body had fallen away. I could see my paralysed limbs, suspended by an energy which held me in place for him to examine me. The moment he settled on the ground a few yards away from me, his nearness triggered something, animating my burn scar, which throbbed slowly with a beautiful penetrating heat. His smile grew, beaming at me in disbelief. The dry cracks in his dark brown skin turned into canyons as his smile squeezed tears from his eyes that found their channels in his face like the first rains blessing a parched riverbed. He swirled his blanket around his head in one swift movement, unfurling it perfectly in front of him. He smoothed both arms across it in a breaststroke motion, briefly resting his forehead on the fabric before sitting up with his shining smile.

I realised then that no words would be exchanged, which was fortunate as I couldn't use my tongue. He reached for a small, light-brown leather bag hanging from his neck; its top was secured with a drawstring thread which he loosened before holding the bag open over the blanket, waiting. His other hand beckoned back and forth at the bag's opening, an action immediately accompanied by a deep humming from his pursed lips. He looked up and winked at me mischievously. The throbbing beats of my scar grew stronger with every note he hummed. The tune was so familiar, like a nursery rhyme I'd heard thousands of times, sending me to sleep. The first movements in the bag were slight yet strong, stretching the thin leather to the brink of bursting. A small white skull forced itself out, tumbling onto the blanket. My breathing quickened as the rhythm of my scar grew stronger: boom, boom, boom!

With the release of the skull, the pitch of his humming lifted and fell in an enchanting melody. If the flight of a bird could be sung, it would sound like his song. I had heard it before. Every note coaxed a succession of bones from the bag, some short, some long, some no bigger than a finger nail. He kept glancing at me as he sang, waving his open palm at the small bag to bring all the bones to rest on the blanket. The final note hung effortlessly on the forest air, reverberating, with no desperateness for breath. The final bone fell from the bag at the precise moment he stopped singing. And there they rested. The skull was now buried under a pile of bones inches high.

He immediately looked to the sky and as I finally drew my attention away from him I noticed the forest had become dark. Where small gaps of blue sky had once been visible through the canopy, now there were dark grey masses of rolling clouds. The wind whistled through the trees and I knew innately I had to take my place on the blanket next to the giant Indian. I lay on my stomach, burying my face in the blanket, where my nose inhaled the sweet smell of sage. I felt the brief brushing of the back of his fingers as he spread the bones over my back with the gentleness of a priest preparing his altar.

'Howooooo, Howooooo!!!' he cried, over and over again. I braced myself, gripping the blanket like a baby refusing to surrender its rag comforter. I heard the crack before the light cut into my back. The sound of a hundred whiplashes bounced off the trees like a pinball machine. At first, the shock denied me the pain, but not for long.

'Howooooooo!!!' We screamed together; the agony of a hot metal rod being shoved up my spine shot through my body. I looked up at him for help, only to meet his lips as they kissed my forehead. His huge hands helped me rest my head on its side, and the smell of sage replaced that of my burning skin – a smell I knew all too well. I started to lose consciousness, the forest floor spun, I watched his bare feet walk away from me and as the most beautiful sound I could ever remember hearing filled my ears, 'Caw! Caw! Caw!', the lights behind my eyes went out.

ELEVEN

I didn't return to the mountain for several days. Opportunities arose to visit Newlands again, but it took me a while to process what happened in the forest. My body and mind were cleaner than they'd been for years, so his face remained with a sharpness I'd never known my memories to have. The forest 'trip' threw me off balance, distracting me from my programme. I spent more time sitting on the edge of the terrace smoking, staring at the owl, watching Crow obliterate pigeons and writing a two-thousand-word essay on punctuality and planning as a consequence for returning from Newlands two hours late. My head wasn't always the quietest or most rational place, but it was finding balance for the first time in years. I retreated from everyone again, preferring to soak in the presence of the Indian's face and to welcome the frequent daydream of Crow's huge black wings opening behind me to envelop me with their huge span.

I was quieter around the community, which drew

unwanted attention during group meetings where raising 'concerns' for each other's behaviour put someone in a glaring spotlight of attention. The meetings were held in a small room off the kitchen just big enough for the community and counsellors to sit snugly next to each other. I soon got used to other people being near me by default; it was impossible to avoid the brushing of arms or legs and eventually I just surrendered again. Resistance was futile, and exhausting. Letting go of all the little insecurities once hidden behind a wall of false drug-induced confidence became a more learned and natural response.

'I'd like to start. I have concern for Aaron. He's isolating, gone quiet. I hear from some of the other guys he's not sharing at meetings, either. We ask you to try and share at every meeting, Aaron. But you're flying under the radar. What's up?' Clarke said.

He was the only other male counsellor apart from Troy. I liked his South African afro and I respected him, just as I respected the whole counselling team. I had such huge respect for their desire to help others, and while I kept an honest programme I couldn't risk telling the whole community about my other-worldly adventure. My taught, hunched body language telegraphed my angst.

'I've got itchy feet, I feel like leaving but I know it's the worst thing I can do,' I said. Not a bad response and not too far from the truth.

'Why don't you let the anger out?' Clarke said.

'What anger?'

'I think you're keeping it inside, Aaron, and it won't do you any good. Go take it out on the punch bag in the garden.'

'I'm not angry!' I white-knuckled my fists hidden under my legs. Something stirred inside me: something uncomfortable. Clarke had pushed a button I'd kept hidden away for a long time. I'd never been in a fight with anyone except a few flashes of temper towards my brother and sisters when I was twelve years old. While they were few and far between, I knew the intensity of my anger had the potential to maim, or worse. I'd narrowly missed spearing my sister with a metal pole which stuck into her bedroom door as she disappeared screaming behind it.

There was anger inside me, but more than that. When I thought about never having any scraps at school like some of the other lads, I realised it wasn't because I was passive or afraid, it was because I felt like if it were worth fighting, then fight to the death. I felt a fury sleeping, ancient and yet so familiar. I told one of the counsellors about the flashes of extreme psychotic violence I'd felt close to, flicking the worst fuck-it switch and attacking my friends with a kitchen knife. The sickness conspired to bring me down and leave a hateful legacy. The end of the marriage was one way to keep her safe.

'Are you angry at Karen for divorcing you? Or perhaps at yourself for betraying her? Maybe you're angry at this disease?' Clarke poked suggestions at me.

'It's the disease. I hate what it's done to me and my marriage,' my response was quick, and true. After years of lying to myself and my family, sobriety's default setting was honesty, and right then I felt the deep pain of remorse for how I'd dirtied our wedding vows. Missing the marriage was not an option; it was shattered beyond repair and I had no right to miss the love I'd dirtied, but a sense of freedom slowly enveloped me. I didn't know if I had the right to feel free, but it was undeniable, and exciting.

'For sure,' Clarke seemed familiar with my response.

'I've taken any anger towards this disease out on that punch bag out there. I nearly broke my foot I kicked it so hard. D'ya really think I'm flying under the radar after all the fucking crying I've done?' I said.

Kicking the bag always felt forced. I was frustrated at the counsellor's expectation that everyone in rehab had some anger they needed to express. Claustrophobia smothered me. I left the room bringing inevitable consequences my way. I sat cross-legged on the grass at the bottom of the garden and rested my head in my hands, letting the energy flow through me, carried on the waves of unidentifiable emotions. Getting to know myself again was a simple process. Listen, surrender, pray, show up, let go and pray some more. But it was never going to be easy. As I stage-dived into the therapeutic process I knew the counsellors would catch me, and they did. I was ready for therapy, but it was the awakening of my spirit I wasn't prepared for.

Soft, slow footsteps followed behind me through the grass. 'You know, Aaron,' Troy said as he sat next to me, 'some people come here, get better and carry on with their old lives as best they can. They make minor adjustments to their lifestyles, staying clean most of the time, but they keep living the same existence they did before rehab. Never realising they're in the wrong relationship or job, and they can't find that extra bit of courage to take a leap of faith and make the biggest change they know they need to. They're too scared to completely let go of an old way of life that never served a positive purpose. Others make this an opportunity to turn the tables on the disease and let themselves be catapulted into the unknown beauty of a new life to answer a calling. That, my friend, is you! They've been waiting a long time for you to get here.'

'Who are you talking about?' I said.

'You've met one of them already.' Troy pointed at Crow, pecking for grubs in the grass.

'I hear and see a lot, Aaron, more than I wanted to when I was a kid, much like you. Being psychic can be a curse if you don't know how to close it down or channel it in the right direction. Using drugs was the only way I knew how to protect myself from sensory overload. I was quite happy with my bag of prescription pills; everyone felt so sorry for me. It suited me just fine. It's a great way of shutting out the world or showing them who you really aren't, eh, my friend?' Troy smiled and put his hand on my shoulder. 'Know how I got this?' He pointed to the burn scar on his neck.

'How?'

'I was walking in Newlands Forest ten years ago, thirty days clean, proud of myself and just listening to the mountain. She spoke to me then. You have Crow, I have Owl. I would've been readmitted if I told them the story, and how the stones and trees reached out to me; they called out, not with a human voice, but with this... vibe!'

I looked at Troy, stunned. 'I hear a drum beat coming from her. It started out like a distant, whirring hum, and then the closer I got the more the rhythm and the beat showed itself to me. I call it Mother's heartbeat.'

'I know, Aaron, she calls out to some of us in different ways. I sat back against a tree and shut my eyes for I don't know how long; it doesn't take long for her to change the weather around her. Sometimes Mother just wants a bit of privacy so she brings in the cloud, rain and wind to keep everyone away. We all like our privacy when we're having a shower eh? Nothing wrong with that. She must've brought it in pretty quick 'cos I missed the sunshine hiding; I remember hearing this 'crack' as the lightning struck the tree and wrapped me in its charge. My eyes stung like hell. I was blind for two days; the doctors told me the lightning melted the clothes to my skin. We're not strangers, Aaron. The scars on your back and on mine speak the same language. We've both had the same initiation from the fire of heaven. It's the closest you'll get to being initiated.'

'Initiated into what?' I said.

'Working with the Spirits. They're asking you to trust them, to listen to what they're asking of you. They've been nudging you, preparing you, guiding you all your life for this time and for what's to come.' He looked up to the sky with his arms falling out to the side, palms facing upwards.

'What do they want me to do? What's coming?'

'That's between you and them, no one else. Sometimes our ancestors wait hundreds of years for the one person to come along who is willing to walk the path with them. This material world is just a thin veil in which we function to no more than one percent of our true power and potential. The Spirit world is where some of us excel. Your guides have been telling you all your life, you just couldn't hear them until now and you see so clearly, don't you?'

'Yes, I see in the dark now. When I close my eyes and listen to Mother's heartbeat my head spins and I'm transported somewhere else, somewhere so new to me and yet it feels like coming home.' Emotion surged from my heart, and tears began to burst through, a silence befell the garden and distracted me. Life paused for a moment, and Troy's pupils rolled back in his head, showing only whiteness staring out from his brown skin.

'Aaron, we wouldn't be sitting here talking if it weren't for divine intervention of some kind. You've nearly finished a treatment programme for drug addiction, a spiritual programme. You need to shed your skin of this old, tired way of living and exchange it for an awakening. This is what everything you notice is all about. Your path can take you to lands many only dream of seeing. This is a crossroads for you. Behind you wait madness and death. To the left and right the one-dimensional life of conformity keeps you grounded, but straight ahead is a life beyond your wildest dreams, full of light, magic, wonderment and love the likes of which cannot be described, only felt with the language of the heart and seen through the eyes of Spirit. You have those eyes, Aaron. When the moon's face next shines full, go to the highest place on the Mother's rock and all will be made clear for you to choose your direction. You can see now that this is your moment in life to surrender your soul to nature; your soul is entwined with the Spirits now. It offers you great knowledge. Plant your roots deep below you to the centre of this earth where the volcanic fires burn brightly and you shall soar. You share the same soul with Crow up there in the tree. In a lifetime long ago you lived as an American Indian and were able to hear the wisdom of the Crow. A strong bond was formed between the two of you. Your fates were forever sealed as sharing each lifetime in harmony to expand into greater awareness. Crow appeared when you were ready to accept. You may have believed that you were connecting with many different crows, but in truth it is just one. He says you are his half-brother. He brings you great wisdom and when you are ready, he will speak the truth of the ages. You will not struggle to hear it, for it will just be known within you. Crow is a part of you. You are truly blessed.'

Troy's eyes returned to his head. 'Hmmm. Whatever was said then was for you, Aaron, but remember this when you start to wonder this new path. We all hail from indigenous roots, whether they are American Indian, Scandinavian, or a blend of several ancient traditions, but the noise of life beyond this garden and the symptoms of disconnection, like addiction, can distract us from our more intuitive, indigenous ways of knowing and being. For you, yes, it is crucial you remember your ancestors and where you came from, but in this life too! To explore your Celtic origins, that is what will bring you the most fulfilment and ultimately greatness! There is no doubt, Aaron, you have so much ahead of you and soon you will have a very big decision to make.'

Troy gently squeezed my shoulder, stealing a brief stroke of the raised scar tissue under my tee shirt before leaving me to sit and smoke cigarettes in contemplation of what I'd just heard. Fresh tears streamed down my cheeks, but for the first time since treatment began, they didn't carry any sadness.

After two months at Calloway House I was ready to move on, but where to was still being decided. Sandy had seen me for most of my one-to-one sessions. I connected well with her because we were of similar age. There was something between us I'd never be able to put my finger on; in fact I felt something in common with 'The Team' as the counsellors referred to themselves. Not just because I now had recovery in common with them. The depth of trust I had in all of them regarding my own welfare felt like nothing I'd ever had for any friend. They felt like family to me, Mark included, because if anyone had been instrumental in starting the healing process, it was his attention to my detail that had broken the onion skin and let the pent-up tears flow. Calloway House was surrounded by this incredible energy because of the love The Team had for everyone entering the gates. They were all angels in my eyes, saving me from hell to show me heaven on earth.

'You can't refer yourself to Shell Bay, Aaron. Things have changed since Guy moved there and stole the television and sound system to fund his relapse,' Sandy said firmly at the end of my last session with her. My life was still, to some extent, in her hands.

Relapses weren't uncommon at all. No sooner had I got used to seeing a new arrival's face at Cedar Ridge or Calloway House than they decided they needed to go back out and do some more research. Every relapse someone else had was a gift from my higher power, telling me to stay on path. Cassie's phone number was now etched on my mind, the thought of researching her some more still flickering in my head.

So far, I'd escaped the clutches of a disease which tried to kill me. Instead of taking my life, it had brought me to a new country and cleared the fog, helping me see how precious life was. I was seeing life through new eyes, which perceived something deeper in what I used to think was reality. I wanted to learn more about this new path.

I kept my distance from the sports bar. From now on whenever I saw someone drinking alcohol an invisible wall grew between us, transforming the drinker into an alien living a life I could not comprehend. It was a miracle. The desire to drink had been lifted from me and the desire to live life took its place; not even the sweet smell of marijuana wafting over the wall distracted me from the second chance I'd been given. Seven, eight, two… seven, eight, two… the last three digits of Cassie's phone number lulled me to sleep.

My addiction had started with smoking a plant, and then alcoholism had taken its place as I drank the essence of another plant; finally, I'd snorted my way through a plant in powder form. The spirit of plant drove me insane. It intoxicated and blighted every corner of my life. The smell of the pot plant always produced the same brief reaction of euphoria followed by a stark reminder of the terror and wreckage in England. I had a built-in defence mechanism against the illness. That seemed to be the way my body and mind worked at the time, always in surges of emotion or flashes of memory. I was easily unbalanced. Regulating or rationalising my feelings and thoughts was exhausting. I rushed and dipped from zero to a thousand on the Richter scale in seconds.

Sandy reminded me I wasn't ready to make decisions regarding my own treatment progression. Of course, I could just tell them all to go fuck themselves and go home with a resentment against them in my bag, which would jump out at me when I unpacked my ill-equipped toolbox for living normally, to relapse into the bitterness. But I chose to be patient and the next day I was told I could move to Shell Bay for a few weeks of step-down.

Shell Bay was a former guest house converted into a treatment facility by Henrick; people stayed here as a last port of call before going home. It was also known as

Tertiary or step-down. Some said it was like being on holiday, and compared to primary or secondary, it was. Group counselling sessions happened once a week; I had the freedom to make it to my own meetings as and when I wanted, which was the most responsibility for my own life I'd had since coming to South Africa.

Christmas was a bizarre affair in Cape Town. The shopping malls played carols which clashed with the African sunshine and soaring temperatures. It felt awful and for most of the British contingent at Calloway it brought on a severe bout of homesickness.

On Christmas Eve I took the train with Jimmy to Camps Bay Beach. We were quiet with each other. The reality of why we weren't spending Christmas with our families hit home, or maybe it was the realisation that Christmas would never be the same again, no matter where we spent it. The partying used to start weeks before Christmas Day, so when Christmas finally came I was so sleep-deprived and obsessed with scoring enough cocaine for New Year's Eve that the time of year lost all its childhood meaning. My last Christmas was spectacularly awful, but I'd had a very good one, totally buzzed off my arse and almost camouflaged by the surrounding contagious seasonal excess. Christmas took on a new meaning for me. As I thought about the little fella in the manger being born, I was having a reincarnation of my own.

Jimmy and I were the only people occupying the graffiti-ridden carriage, which made me feel uneasy. We were told never to travel on the trains alone as muggings were commonplace on public transport. Still, I'd gone three months without seeing any crime which strengthened the sense of Spirit's force-field, keeping me safe. We retreated back to our thoughts.

I kept watch for any glimpses of Mother from the train. Her cauldron brewed its magic and the Cape Doctor cooled her scorching rock. I phased my vision in and out from the scenery to my reflection, comparing it to the last photo taken of me before I left England with my thin head sucked dry of happy thoughts. In the window I saw someone new, strong and rejuvenated, another stranger, but one I looked forward to becoming acquainted with.

Still a little unsteady on my recovered feet, I had two big decisions to make in the next few weeks before treatment finished: when to go home, and when to visit Mother's table-top. I ruled out walking the four-hour trail from Newlands Forest. Some days my pace was reduced to a hobble as I limped in pain from my drinking injuries which I accepted as I accepted so many of the other consequences. My foot would heal, everything would in time, but for now the pain was a reminder of the past and also a deterrent. I found gratitude for every working part of my body. The fact that my liver was unscathed didn't make any sense, but I wasn't complaining of yet another miracle.

I heard an adjoining carriage door open, followed by the rustle of plastic bags as their owner found her seat. An orange rumbled across the floor to me, diverting my gaze from Mother to return the fruit to its owner who was waiting with the biggest smile. It was the very same smile I'd seen at the level crossing months ago: the woman I'd helped to her feet and whose blood I had on my hands had found me again. 'Thank you,' she said, keeping eye contact. 'You're welcome,' I replied. I hadn't yet mastered the art of striking up conversation with strangers, and unspoken mutual appreciation negated the need for any more words. The woman put her orange back in the bag and began singing a song which sent shivers down my spine and sprang every hair on my body. 'Amen, Amen, Alleluia, Amen, Amen...' Just two words in the most beautiful voice – and really, this was the first time in my life I was actually hearing anything with clean, sober senses channelling the beauty right to my soul. Lifting it high. A fire burned inside me, combusting, turning the pistons powering my spiritual engines. I'd navigated some of the rockiest seas and now Mother's rock stood proud, a beacon guiding me to the sacred land, to the Spirit world.

'Getting close, isn't it,' Jimmy said, pushing himself up on his elbows as we extended our tanning competition on the egg-timer sand of Camps Bay. His flightiness had calmed considerably; he managed to roast on the sand for nearly half an hour before he sprinted to the ice-cold Atlantic for an ankle-numbing dip. His time had finally come to leave Cape Town that evening.

'What's that, Jimmy?'

'Going home. It could only be a few weeks if Shell Bay goes well for you. I've got a list of meetings for the South

London area; I'll leave it on your bed.'

'Thanks, Jimmy,' I said, tensely gripping two fists of sand at the thought of returning to the scene of my crimes, and to a job I was disenchanted with. 'How are ya feeling about going back?'

'Not sure, it'll be weird. I miss my kids so much, but the restraining order hasn't gone away so I don't know when I'll get to see 'em. I can only hope she'll see I've changed,' he said, slipping his shades over his eyes and reclining back on the sand, not a twitch in sight.

Jimmy had certainly changed; his hyperactivity had dissolved with every passing day. I was glad there would be someone waiting for me in England who knew what I'd been through in rehab: someone who understood exactly how straight and narrow the new way to live needed to be.

'Comply or die, buddy, comply or die.' Jimmy repeated his motto, inhaling an extra-long Marlboro Light in one hand and a granadilla ice-lolly in the other. 'Don't waste any time getting in touch when you come home, Aaron. I'll be a hermit when I get home; remember, change the people, places and things. Meetings are where we'll find like-minded people. They don't call it the fellowship for nothing.'

'Huh, okay, Jimmy.'

An afternoon of beach volleyball sapped both our desires to make conversation. I drifted in and out of sleep, occasionally sitting up like a meerkat in response to Jimmy's gift for locating one of the multitude of stunning bikini-clad girls visiting from Johannesburg for the

Christmas break, but increasingly I wanted to be left alone to dwell in the quieter depths of my mind that I was exploring for the first time. I avoided thinking about returning to England, replaying the unsettling warning my sister had given me whenever I thought about seeing my parents again.

'I think you should know, Mum isn't sure she can have you living back at home,' she'd said. It was a fair but unhelpful point to make – emphasised by the twenty-two pages of collateral from my family which I'd barged my way through every damages session to share. As I descended into the brief stillness offered to me on the beach, a light-bulb moment showed me that I had to make amends to myself as well as to my family. One couldn't happen without the other. The first thing I did when I returned to Calloway House that day was call my dad to tell him I was staying on for a final month of treatment.

'Aaron, you need to remember, we'll have you back however you come,' he said. I couldn't understand the depth of love his words expressed to me, but for the first time I caught a glimpse of how much a parent could love their child. I put the phone down, holding my dad in awe. Recovery was so new and relationships were already becoming richer.

As I watched Jimmy leave Calloway House in the taxi, I knew I'd outgrown the second stage of treatment. Cravings for drugs and alcohol still hadn't returned. I didn't know if they ever would, or if I'd manage to stay clean in the long run, but my recovery had got off to a good start even if I had been sidetracked by Cassie. I was still clean.

Darren chose a different path, or perhaps he actually woke up himself. Rehab never suited him. He always seemed too fucking happy to be in rehab. I couldn't see any pain or remorse in him. He just seemed like a kid who got mixed up with the wrong crowd, who bundled him into a sack to scare the living shit out of him; he was just a scared kid, last seen on Facebook bragging about the delights of Leffe Beer and a fancy malt whisky. Rehab was a safe haven for him and there was nothing wrong with that.

With my departure for Shell Bay imminent, I walked into the garden at dusk to say goodbye to the place where I'd spent so many mornings getting to know myself and my higher power. The evening dew cleansed my feet as they brushed through the thick grass. Crow and Owl shared the same high branch, perched closely next to each other.

'Twoo!'

'Caw!'

After saying my prayers of gratitude, I was suddenly overcome with sorrow for all the pain Karen and my family had endured because of the path I took to get to Cape Town. I walked to the flower beds, searching for the most beautiful flower, one which reminded me of Karen's beauty and my love for her. When I found it, I laid it gently where I usually sat, and let her go.

I had no trouble adjusting to the freedom of Shell Bay.

I was one of six people. We mostly kept ourselves to ourselves save a little morning and evening banter in the kitchen at mealtimes. Occasionally we were all roused at night by Teresa screaming at hallucinations of a man in her room. She was an adorable seventy-three-year-old Irish lady disowned and shipped off to Cape Town by her family. I half expected her hallucinations to make me feel uneasy at night, having just got used to sleeping in a room on my own after Jimmy's departure, but I wasn't rattled. I loved the adrenalin buzz when I heard her scream. Some nights I'd just leave the others to it and stare at the darkened corners of my bedroom, watching the air shine and sparkle with golden energy. Other times, as I sent myself to sleep channelling the energy through my palms to my chest to try and heal my chemically burnt lungs, the room lit up in patches of yellow light surrounded by swirling shadows, and the room swam with paranormal activity. I had no fear of it anymore, only fascination.

I put off going anywhere near Table Mountain for the first three weeks of Shell Bay. Bizarrely, as soon as I was given the freedom to go wherever I wanted, I chose the beach every day. Shell Bay was in the aptly named area, Table View. It was notorious for kitesurfing-winds which sand-blasted my skin every time I tried to chill on the beach. The view of Mother and her children was at its most spectacular from my new neighbourhood, especially from the huge open-plan living space on the first floor where full-length windows stretched the length of the building providing access to a long balcony. The converted guest house felt luxurious with en suite bathrooms and the central-feature fireplace and widescreen television which the deep sofas focused on. My drives from Shell Bay to any of the Clifton or Camps Bay beaches gave me the most beautiful profile of the table-top. Every time I looked at the summit butterflies fluttered madly in my stomach. I had no idea what was waiting for me, but it'd been there since childhood: a feeling of being part of something big and vital.

Crow kept his distance, sitting on the same brown sign for the Table Mountain Cable Car, waiting for me every day as I drove to the beach. I hid myself there, baking my skin brown and savouring the sight of girls walking wet out of an ocean which teemed with schools of dolphin and the occasional humpback whale breaching half a mile out to sea. As the penultimate week of treatment drew to a close moments of blind panic started warning me not to miss what could be a once in a lifetime opportunity to visit the top of the mountain. I had no idea where my life was leading me. Acceptance was the key – the answer to all my problems, they told me. I'd learnt that not only was I a good person, but that I had something golden inside me to share with a world which was starting to appear much bigger, deeper and more multi-dimensional than society had conditioned me to believe.

I no longer needed to change the way I felt with drugs and alcohol to fit in, because I realised fitting in was the last thing I needed to do. By listening to the similarities of what people had to say in the meetings I knew I wasn't alone and that in fact, while membership to Alcoholics Anonymous didn't cost any money, it had the highest price of mental, emotional and physical pain to pay for entry. I was now a member of the one of the largest spiritual organisations in the world. The disease which had tried to kill me also cleansed me. It cleared the fog and opened my eyes. By returning from the edge of life and death, I set my soul free.

At seven o'clock in the morning on the third day before my flight back to England I drove my hire car to the cable car station. Since moving to Shell Bay, I'd developed something of a cross addiction to buying music. Sobriety had opened my ears, and my car was littered with compact discs, but that morning I didn't feel like playing anything. As I stepped into the car I paused, one foot inside and one still outside on the ground. I rested my arms on the roof of the car to listen to the power of the Table View wind as it whistled through the telephone cables and the metal bars of the security gate, shaking the palm trees. Time stood still, and I heard Troy tell me he was 'so excited!' I glanced at Mother in the distance with my first taste of pure adrenalin: a buzz so clean, no drink or drug came close to the exhilaration.

My mind was clear and uncluttered by the speculation of when and where my next fix or drink would come from. My sensitivities grasped the sights and sounds of the Great Outdoors. I felt so strong and proud of myself that day and even through nature's howl, I heard Mother's heart calling me from fifteen miles away.

'Boom! Boom!' she said, but I'd forgotten to hold onto the car door and a sandy gust forced my head to turn and my eyes to shut. I opened my eyes again to see the door slamming down on my ankle. My reactions would never have stopped it in time. I screwed my eyes shut again, bracing myself for the bone-crunching impact, but it never came. When I opened my eyes the car door rested inches away from my ankle. The wind still pushed against the door, but something held it away long enough for me to catch it with my hand and step inside the car.

I arrived at the cable station with a small group of German and Japanese tourists for the first ascent of the day. I was determined to explore the top with as few people as possible. The glass car revolved three-sixty degrees taking me close to Mother's green-grey skin. I felt her breath, her power, so close to me. One minute presented me with a view of the entire Western Cape and the next of Mother's breathing, throbbing skin.

The usual tourist cafe and souvenir shop enticed us to stay near the manmade perimeters of the mountain with walkways and parapets to take in the views overlooking Lion's Head and Signal Hill. I could see the stretch of Camps Bay beach where I'd spent so much time laying still, throwing Frisbee, punching volleyballs, sand-diving and enjoying the female plenty, but I wanted to take myself away from everyone again and find intimacy with Mother.

I headed towards Maclears Beacon, the point where she stretched closest to the heavens, with no idea how long the walk would take, equipped with a pack of cigarettes, a couple of litres of water and a flapjack. The sun had free reign of the sky, but there was no telling what weather Mother would bring in. The terrain soon lost the brick-paved facade and exposed her raw, rough beauty.

Platteklip Gorge, marked as one of the most popular walking routes to the top, cut deep into the table and narrowed to a three-metre-wide dip. I lowered myself down, gripping onto metal chains spiked into the rock, and then hauled myself to table level again, picking up the pace, determined to have as much time alone as possible. The terrain was unpredictable, with pot holes, ponds and tall grassed areas speckling Mother's back. I fixed my vision intensely on the ground and found a good rhythm, pounding my feet until I finally reached the piles of rocks at the Beacon.

The next cigarette felt good as I perched on an outcrop, inhaling the smoke through the clean high air as I recovered from the exertion of the walk. The sun seared my freshly shaved scalp; the wind was nowhere to be heard. Distant mountain ranges called for my attention. I softened my focus, staring through the smoke as I let it slowly pour out of my mouth, drawing it up my nose for a second nicotine hit. I stubbed out the cigarette and put the butt in my pocket. I saw the opportunity to send Reiki to my return to England in the pure surrounding air and began to draw the symbols with my hand, whispering their sacred names to keep them from even the rocks below me. My eyes started flickering slowly at first, but by the end of the final symbol they had rolled back into my skull and fire-like heat filled the space between my cupped hands. The vision came slowly. There was salt in the air followed by sudden bursts of seaweed as the wind roared into my ears. My feet stood on uneven marshy ground which spread out to giant brown-grassed walls of land. I tuned into my body sitting in the sun as it rocked from side to side like a metronome as Mother's energy shot up my spine. My sight finally opened wide through the portal. The land rose steeply in front of me, curved and high, like a tidal-wave about to break. Tick-tock, tick-tock: I rocked back and forth, desperate to see more of the landscape. Mother turned me in a circle to show me that the land was the same in all directions; long sweeping ridges of various heights surrounded me. I was at the centre of a series of circles. A gust of wind threw more salt, seaweed and scents of moist land at me in an avalanche of sensory overload as my vision launched like a rocket into space where I caught a snapshot, from thousands of miles above the earth, of a series of concentric natural circles all framed by the sea. The first sight of the smooth circular shapes was as inspiring as my introduction to Mother's perfect table-top.

The sound of tumbling rocks ended the vision abruptly, making my jumpiness clearly visible to the man trespassing on my journey.

'Sorry to disturb you,' he said in a thick Scottish accent, the movements of his lips hidden by a bushy ginger beard. My anger subsided once I saw his knobbly wooden walking staff, weathered khaki backpack and dented metal canteen, identifying him as a hardened hiker clearly in awe of the view.

'No worries,' I said, dropping the stone I'd instinctively grasped to hurl at the trespasser. I closed my eyes again to find the remnants of the circle's image and keep it imprinted on my mind for as long as possible.

'Beautiful view, eh? Nearly as spectacular as the Highlands,' he chuckled.

'I wouldn't know,' I replied, agitated at his persistence to ruffle my feathers. 'Where are you from then?' I said, giving in to his friendliness.

'Fort William, not far from Glen Coe. Legend has it there's giants living in our Scottish mountains.'

'Legend has it Table Mountain is Mother Nature's home,' I said.

'Hehe, I wouldn't be surprised. Sure is beautiful. Fancy a wee dram?' he said, twisting the lid off his canteen. The smell of whisky hit me instantly.

'No thanks, I don't drink.'

'Whoah! What, never?' he said, losing his footing on a loose rock from the shock.

'Nope, I had one very long party. I drank so much I don't need to drink anymore,' I said, proud of my unrehearsed answer.

'Well, I never did…' He was lost for words. 'Best be off then. Enjoy the rest of your day,' he said, stroking his beard in bewilderment.

'You too.'

I savoured the solitude of the mountain again as he

departed, taking momentary breaks from the view to bask in the sweltering heat, determined to catch as many rays as possible before returning to England's February weather.

'Well done, sir!' Crow's distant voice made me jump a second time, but I was so glad to see him as his wings slowed his landing like a beautiful black parachute.

'Where the hell have you been?'

'Letting you work a few things out, like, how to say 'no' when you're offered a drink,' he said, hopping onto my bent knees, constantly adjusting his balance to avoid scratching the thin skin with his razor-sharp claws.

'So tell me, brother, why are you still here with me?'

'Troy's cool, isn't he? I would've told you eventually, if you stayed clean which, to be honest, looked uncertain back at the barbers.'

'But why do you care?' I said, sparking up another cigarette.

'Because, once, you cared enough to save my life. It'll come back to you some day. I'm not going to spoil all the surprises. I'm just returning the favour. You gotta remember, though, when you start messing around with Reaper, tempting relapse, I go schizo! Don't take what Troy told you for granted, Aaron. Our connection is more than skin-deep, get me?' He flew onto my back and lightly pecked my scar. The circle of land fired into my head as his beak touched my shirt.

'Thanks for keeping me company,' I said, blowing a cloud of cigarette smoke into his face as he returned to my knees.

'No sweat, what are brothers for? Ready for the flight home?' Crow took a drag of the cigarette-cloud and exhaled it through his small nostrils. It was the coolest thing I'd ever seen.

'Not really, I don't know if I can stay clean. Part of me doesn't want to take the risk of hurting my parents again, but another part knows they'd be proud of me if they saw how I've changed. The thought of going back to social work scares the shit out of me, though what else can I do?'

'You made the decision to come out here and clean up your act; you can make the next decision, Aaron. I don't have all the answers. I'll never desert you though. I'm with you 'til the end of time bro'.' Crow took another drag of my smoke, he hopped backwards with his wings spread wide and drifted out of sight.

I explored my feelings and emotions, now so raw. Whenever the pendulum swung towards England I felt nauseous, but if I contemplated staying in Cape Town, I felt tense and knew I would be hiding. I stared out towards the mountain ranges, a far-off land where no one knew me. A fresh start.

I picked up a small stone from the ground, asking for Mother's blessing to take it with me in the hope it would help me decide what to do. The smell of salt caught my nostrils one more time and the curved banks of land lingered in my head as the rotating cable car took me back to the car park. The Scotsman with the bushy beard climbed the steps into his blue and white tour bus. A huge logo of a man tossing a caber adorned half the bus, with the travel operator's title, 'Highland Fling', on the other half. The man waved at me as he took his window seat. I smiled and saluted him.

The top of my head began buzzing with energy as I drove back to Shell Bay. I decided to give a local radio station a chance in the hope I'd find some Bob Marley, but a dance track mixing bagpipes with techno blurted out at full volume, making me swerve into the kerb as I fumbled with the dials to turn down the volume and regain my concentration.

Shell Bay was empty when I arrived. Everyone had gone to a meeting, so I logged on to the internet to check emails and flight times, resigned to the fact that returning to London was the sensible thing to do. An email from Jimmy lifted my spirits as I remembered he was waiting for me to rekindle our friendship, but as I clicked on the subject heading 'Hey' my heart sank.

'Aaron, I'm sorry I won't, no, can't be here when you get home. I was stupid to think I could make it. I need another miracle, but I've used them all up. I can't go back. Maybe I'll come and haunt you one day. God bless. Always your friend. Jimmy.'

A mixture of anger and sadness hit me as I exploded with emotion. I thumped the keyboard, picking the laptop up with both hands, ready to destroy the messenger, but I couldn't give in to the anger; I knew I'd feel defeated picking up the broken pieces. I'd just spent four months picking up my own shattered life. It was time to move forward, not dwell on Jimmy's shattered body as it lay under a motorway bridge. My tears cleared quickly; I was determined to focus on the future without letting the past define me. I moved to the balcony with the laptop; my clattering had opened Google. I looked at Mother. She changed colours in the sun starting its descent over Lion's Head; every sunset was a lightshow worth catching. I was confused and daunted at the thought of going home to attend a friend's funeral, and to a job that had lost its enchantment. The temptation to travel spontaneously and see how long the money from the divorce would last me grew steadily. Mother flashed the circles of land back at me in glorious technicolour. I wondered what could've made such shapes in the land and began searching the internet for anything from crop circles to ancient geometric shapes. The word 'volcano' jumped out at me with bells and whistles on it. I typed one final guess into the search window, 'volcanoes of the British Isles', and there it was. The image I'd seen on my journey: the Ardnamurchan volcano on one of the wildest parts of the Scottish coast, at the most westerly tip of the United Kingdom mainland. The series of rings were the remains of an extinct volcano that last erupted one million years ago.

'That's it! That's it!' a choir of voices bellowed as I clicked on the images. I looked behind me to check the blank screen of the television. The room was quiet, but the sound of my heartbeat pounded away. I closed my eyes and listened intently to the life inside me.

'Boom! Boom!'

TWELVE

The plane's screaming engines lifted me into the sky. I pressed my nose and forehead against the small, oval shaped window in a desperate attempt to catch a farewell glimpse of Table Mountain, and the beaches where I'd laid myself bare to the healing South African elements. My heart felt so heavy; I expected the captain to announce he was turning the plane back to Cape Town due to excess weight. I ran my fingers over the smooth skin of my palms to banish any lingering memory of the illness which had brought me to somewhere I now called my spiritual home.

'I'm sorry,' I whispered to my body as I touched the rim of my nose where sunburnt skin replaced the dents made by a pint glass. I flexed my toes and rubbed the small nodules of healed bone on my once fractured ribs. I remembered the Hawaiian healing prayer we'd been taught at Calloway House and focused it on my body.

'I'm sorry, please forgive me, thank you, I love you,' I prayed over and over again. Asking for my body to forgive me for all the pain I had put it through. Something started to shift inside me. The first hints of respite from the guilt I'd put on my shoulders lightened the load a little. The longer I said the prayer, the lighter I felt. The chip I once had on my shoulder for the rest of humanity disappeared.

'There's no cure for addiction, only a way to arrest it, but when we ask for a daily reprieve the gifts of a new life start flowing in.' Troy's words drifted back to me as the plane levelled out and the seatbelt signs switched off. The disease was lurking right next to me in the form of an oversized man with a cherry-red nose, he was squashed into the seat next to me. He ordered a double whisky-and-ginger for elevenses. His flabby arm overflowed into my seat from the boundary of his arm-rest, occasionally touching mine. I felt a fleeting anxiety about whether I could be infected by his demeanour and returned to the window as we broke through the first layer of cloud. The white veil covered Robben Island as we climbed towards the heavens. I wondered about Mandela and his walk to freedom, and how I had escaped my own prison, but this was no time to feel heavy hearted. I felt excited about seeing my family again and showing them their new son and brother - the real one.

The unfiltered sun streamed onto my face, catching me unawares. I pulled down the shutter, closed my eyes and flicked through memories of the last four months. I beamed a smile of accomplishment as sleep and dream found me.

I heard the sound first. A gentle, rhythmic tapping of

metal hitting metal. Tap, tap, tap… tap, tap, tap. The silvery shapes followed, rising out of the darkness of my mind like a marlin swimming up from the depths of the sea. The blurred image became clearer with every repetition of the rhythm, drawing me further into trance. Three fingers clad in an armoured glove, relentlessly hammered small circular dents into a large metal shield - the owner of the glove had been waiting a long time. The fingers stopped suddenly, the hand lifted up, curling its index finger in my direction back-and-forth, beckoning me to come closer. I felt turbulence shaking my body, calling me back to consciousness. The armoured glove clenched into a fist and rapped its knuckles hard on the shield in frustration. The metal echo synchronised with the ding of the seatbelt sign as the stewardess politely asked me to buckle up. I sniffed the sleeve of my tee shirt, searching for the origin of the sea-salt smell which filled my nostrils once again.

I drifted in and out of sleep for the remainder of the night-flight, huddled under my blanket as far away from my unconscious whiskey-guzzling neighbour as possible. A collage of visions and sounds on a repeating loop started flowing to me, punctuated by Crow's wings and voice at the beginning and end of each sequence. 'They will nudge you gently in the beginning, Aaron. It is best to stay on path.' Crow said, before his black wing lifted the curtain on the tapping armoured glove. It grew rapidly in volume, reaching sledge-hammer proportions which woke me with a shock, causing me to hit my head against the plane's fuselage. The bash knocked me unconscious again, immediately falling prey to the sequence. Crow's voice leered back into my head. 'It is best to stay on path, Aaron.'

I checked my head for bruising before I cleared customs, hoping to spare my parents the anxiety of seeing their son return from rehab with a head injury. My head was unblemished, only Crow's voice echoed, despite my obsessive use of the Serenity Prayer. I began waving at my parents as soon as I saw them. They were huddled together for strength in numbers, praying the imposter was dead and that their son still lived. Our eyes met briefly, but they kept scanning the constant flow of passengers. My mum looked back at me, then away at the other people. I drew closer. My dad looked me straight in the eye, then away again. Twenty-feet, ten, five, I was waving frantically until I stood still just a few feet away from them with my hands in my pockets.

'Hi guys,' I said. Their jaws dropped. I looked into my dad's big kind brown eyes, as mine filled with tears which were coloured with love for the very first time. I buried my head between them. Coming home had never felt so good.

The weeks before my return to social work were spent at my parents' house. I talked to them openly about the new spiritual programme I was following, to regain their trust again and it worked. I kissed my mum and shook my dad's hand as often as possible. I visited my sister to talk until the small hours about rehab, and my growing urge to hand my notice in. I wanted to get as close to them as possible to make up for lost time, but I grew restless and frequently daydreamed about being on my own with nothing but the land for company. Mother was still calling me.

I went to meetings and chain-smoked cigarettes. I didn't go into my old bedroom, preferring to seek solace in the spare room to avoid any lingering intent from the Four Horsemen. My parents gradually got to know me again, but I felt like a round peg in a square hole as I tried to fit back into a life and town which held so little interest for me. Vivid dreams of Ardnamurchan and the impatient armoured glove visited me every night, nudging me… gently. The dreams roused me for a cigarette before I lulled myself back to sleep by placing my hand over the strong, rhythmic beat of my heart. A sound I had wished to leave me several months ago. Crow kept a respectful distance to let me find a place in my family again. The occasional snail ricocheted off the window at night to remind me he was near.

The night before I was due to go back to work I leant out of the bathroom window with my night-cap of hot chocolate and Marlboro Red. An owl's hoot came from the man in the moon's mouth as he smiled proudly down on me from his home in the sparkling bluey-black sky. My senses were so heightened at night after the background hubbub of the working day had died. I picked up everything. From a mouse's rustle in the hedgerow; to the soft squeaking of a bat as it found its roost, and the pitter-patter of a cat's feet doing the night-shift around its territory. The darkened air teemed with golden energy which had awakened within and all around me. I was less than twelve hours away from returning to the rat race, a choice I realised, right then, would be the wrong one. I knew where I had to go. The lights behind my eyes were brighter than ever.

THE BEGINNING

14014786R00115

Printed in Great Britain
by Amazon.co.uk, Ltd.,
Marston Gate.